A WIFE
FOR MY SON

A WIFE
FOR MY SON

Ali Ghalem

Translated from the French by
G. Kazolias

Banner Press, New York
Africa World Press, Inc.

Originally published as *Une Femme Pour Mon Fils*
© 1979 Editions SYROS 1 rue de Varenne, 75007 Paris

Banner Press, Chicago
Zed Press, London
Cover by Maya Mattei
© 1984 by Banner Press
All rights reserved
Printed in USA

Second printing 1986
Third printing 1988
Fourth printing 1991

A co-publication of Africa World Press, Inc. and
Banner Press

Africa World Press, Inc.

P.O. Box 1892
Trenton, New Jersey 08607
(609) 695-3766

Library of Congress Cataloging in Publication Data

Ghalem, Ali.
    A wife for my son.

        Translation of: Une femme pour mon fils.
        I. Title.
PQ3989.2.G54F413   1984   843   84-20414
ISBN 0-916650-33-2
ISBN 0-916650-17-0 (pbk)

ISBN 0-86543-116-7

I thank all those who enlightened me and made it possible for me to write this book.

*To my mother who died when
I was only a few months old.*

*To my cousin, To my brother,
To my whole family,
To all those who experience these conflicts.*

I.

Fatiha was looking out of the window of the taxi but nothing could take her mind off of what she had just been through at the hammam. Not the bright sunlight, nor the rich blue sky, nor the city she loved, nor the crowd, so dense the people seemed to carry one another along from store to store. The taxi slowed to a stop at an intersection. Just two steps from the Galleries, old women, hidden under their worn cloaks, walked back and forth offering smuggled golden necklaces and rings. Fatiha's eyes focused on two young women wearing veils. They seemed to hang on to the jeweler's window so as not to be pushed away before they could choose or at least admire the jewelry offered to their fancy. Fatiha was struck more than usual by the fact that such young women were wearing veils; one thing was for sure—she would never wear a veil! It symbolized for her the life of a woman in the past and she wanted to live in the present; she did not like this concealing of the face, even if it could be quite useful at times. . .and only over women's faces! Two men noticed the bride-to-be and they smiled with a gesture of appreciation. The taxi started off again, dodging in and out of traffic, avoiding the people who ran into the street without paying the slightest heed to the traffic; horns blasting at them, they arrogantly crossed, a bit argumentative and full of self-satisfaction. The sun beat down on the pavement; a few paupers, squatting against the trees, basked in the sun as if to numb their fate.

Fatiha sat among the talkative, happy women in the taxi taking her back to her parents'. They no longer paid attention to her, content to be chatting together. She thought back to the days when she would go to the baths with her mother. The heat and steam, undressed women moving about with large hips and tired bodies, the superb bodies of the children and young girls, the inquisitive looks of the old matchmakers looking for future fiancées, the joy of lavishly pouring water. The women would vigorously scrub their children and then rub them down with ointments they had secretly made from cloves and lemons churned together which would make the skin so soft. What had once been such a joy had now become frustrating to the point of tears. It was not her mother who had undone her long hair but the skillful old woman charged with the preparation of future brides. She had firmly pinned Fatiha between her legs and washed her hair with deliberation. Fatiha, dazed by the noise of the conversations around her, by the laughing and yelling, the children's arguments, the sweet smell of soap and oranges, had let herself be groomed but not without irritation. Her mother smiled at her but her look expressed some worry.

"Are you happy, dear?"

Fatiha had looked away. The heat, steam, and strong odors; soapy water blurred her vision. The old woman diligently continued her job paying no attention to Fatiha's disposition, but rather to her cleanliness and beauty. She took off her fouta, laid it out on the floor and asked Fatiha to lie on her stomach. Fatiha hesitantly obeyed. The old woman washed her with great tenderness, caressing her as if she wanted to awaken her virgin body to unknown pleasures. Fatiha—naked, embarrassed, choking from the heat, annoyed at being manipulated in this way, stared at, appraised—tensed up that much more under these completely new and unexpected caresses. She was surprised by the rush of anger and rebellion within her; these stubborn sentiments were quite new to her; she could not recall ever being so tense and closed. She sat up suddenly, splashing her masseuse; the masseuse paying no attention, smiled with the satisfaction of a job well done.

"On Saturday the little girl will become a woman! You will be the most beautiful!"

Just then Fatiha caught sight of the handsome face of a young woman she did not know, but who was looking at her gravely and with admiration. The stare was so intense that Fatiha could feel it throughout her body. Then the experienced hand of the old woman made her lie back down on the drenched tiles. Next came the torture of depilation. Torture . . . the word did not seem too strong to Fatiha. This operation, which seemed so necessary and harmless to the old washer of virgins, was very much like torture for her. She slowly applied the cream to her legs and arms, to her pubis and her face. Fatiha held back the tears with clenched fists, pinched lips and contracted muscles.

"Hair is not nice, my pretty; on men it's all right! It makes men beautiful, but us . . . it makes us ugly! That's the way it is."

The old woman laughed.

"We've got to have skin like satin, my pretty, like a flower petal! Your skin will be like silky velvet to please your husband; he will be happy and so will you!"

She then began to sing; the revulsion at being treated in this way was so strong in Fatiha's heart that she could not let the words of the old woman's song carry her away. It became more and more difficult to hold back the tears. Her mother neared:

"Come on, honey, it's almost over . . . and it's not so terrible!" She took her hand delicately.

"My charm, my velvet, you're going to be so beautiful!" The old woman continued her task; she had plucked the excess eyebrows hindering the perfection of the arch and then contemplated her work with satisfaction. Houria, her mother, seemed as satisfied as the old washer; she handed Fatiha her fouta and her slippers; the women demonstrated their admiration and joy by clapping hands and shouting.

But now she was riding through town in a taxi. She felt like she was being led by some unknown force, as if she were walking in her sleep, ignoring her own preferences, fears, and hopes. The women in the taxi chatted, and since they were preparing a wonderful wedding, they chatted about weddings . . .

"They had promised their daughter to Larki when she was only ten years old . . . ten . . . last year they married her to Mahmoud. Babouchi went to her parents' house and shot her father! How horrible! How horrible! But they had promised her to . . . "

The old washer had thrown salt water under Fatiha's feet to ward off the evil spirits. She was deeply moved by the young girl she had just prepared for the wedding and who was being offered the great adventure of marriage . . . as for an adventure . . . that is what it was . . . some get the lucky number, as they say, while others get the wrong one . . . And as usual she recalled her own wedding; fifty years before! Fifty years! You see a lot in fifty years! Births, deaths, weddings and divorces, happiness . . . sorrow . . . that's life! May God grant her many children and spare her from war . . . because war takes your husbands and children; what's the sense in taking great pains to bring them up just to . . . Fatiha remembered the old woman's look as she left, strange, affectionate, gay, and sad all at once, indecipherable. The colors of the town flashed by the window of the taxi, the blankets and wash hanging from windows like flags on a holiday, the red and mauve bougainvillea cascading down the walls, and glimpsed down a side street reflections of the sun over the sea.

The sea! How much more she would have preferred to be swimming and running along the beach than sitting there in the taxi! Did Hocine, her future husband, like the sea? He had lived in France so he just had to be 'modern.' And with the certainty that he was 'modern,' which for her meant that all things were possible, Fatiha let herself daydream. The women next to her continued chatting excitedly about anything and nothing, loquacious, happy to be there together, happy to be part of the celebration.

Hocine, bare-chested, walked out of the steam of the men's bath and lay on the mat. An old masseur with a jovial and slightly mischievous expression approached.

"So, you're getting married, my son?"

Hocine nodded. The masseur leaned towards him solicitously.

"May God grant you peace, my son, and give you beautiful children!"

"Thank you."

"Not too many children. . .children are easy to make, as the saying goes. . .but to bring home the bread is hard. . .right?"

Hocine acknowledged with a smile and let himself go, relaxing under the large and strong hands slowly massaging his back.

"I was married too, and to the best cook in the whole area. That's for sure."

He paused for a moment as if to persuade Hocine and then went back to work.

"Do you like prunes?"

Hocine, lifting himself up on his elbows, turned and

said with a laugh:

"Of course! What a question! Who doesn't like prunes?"

"Well, she was the queen of prunes, that's for sure!"
He stopped massaging again and shook his head slowly:
"She's dead now. She died at Aïd last year. In the morning; just like that, she didn't wake up, left like an angel, my son... like an angel, that's for sure!"

Hocine rolled over and studied the man's face. It was deeply lined with wrinkles revealing not hardness but simplicity and kindness, as well as a touch of mischievousness. The liveliness of his look, passing from a smile to sadness in a matter of seconds, was a little like the the clouds in the French skies, quick, covering the sun before you knew it.

"An honest hardworking wife is God's greatest gift, my son!"

He remained quiet a few minutes, massaging Hocine intently.

"You know something: I don't think I ever loved her as much as I loved her once she passed on..."

He seemed to hesitate.

"Without her... without her... you see my son... without her... it's as if I didn't exist any more... that's for sure!"

"Oh come on now... you look alive enough to me!"

"I'm old. I have a son and a daughter. I had two sons but one died in the war. Yeah... he's dead. We bring children into the world; we raise them with such difficulty and then they die, just like that... He was a good son..."

He continued to massage Hocine with the utmost care.

"I work here three days a week. I am very well cared for by my daughter; I have four grandchildren, two girls and two boys. Ah yes... my son... an honest wife and obedient children are God's greatest gift!"

The old man continued to work in silence. Hocine felt

good. The old man's face suddenly reminded him of his roommate in France, an immigrant worker like himself. Then he experienced a recurring phenomenon. Without reason or warning two distinct moments were being lived at the same time, both with the same intensity: the past and the present, here and elsewhere. He was in the reassuring warmth of the Moorish bath and at the same time in his barely heated room, disagreeably startled by the cold water from the faucet. Steam. Warmth. Moorish bath. His body at ease. Cold, overcome by discomfort. His body contracted. He looks at himself in the broken mirror, disappointed by his tired face. One of his roommates also wakes and begins making coffee, still half asleep. The gentle warmth of the Moorish bath. The old masseur smiling at him. All around them playful voices and laughing. Fog. Cold. Morning dawns on the working class suburbs of Paris. Hocine raises the collar of his overcoat; the far off whistle of a suburban train. A silhouette approaches him:

"Hey, Hocine!"

"Hi."

"How's it goin'?"

"All right."

The platform of a suburban train station. A few familiar faces encountered every day. The face of a young woman with bright, light brown eyes and a soft gaze, like that of a child. And the face of that tired man, always buried in the racing form, looking for the number that will get him out of there. The Moorish bath. Warmth. Happiness. Cold. The hot morning expresso quickly swallowed at the edge of the bar. Sometimes good, sometimes bad. A worker slaps him familiarly on the shoulder.

"Hey! Mohamed!"

"Not Mohamed! Hocine... I've already told you a dozen times!"

"Sorry! Don't take it bad; got no memory, smoke too much they say! Say...6...7...14...who would've guessed that God damned nag 14? Eh Mo...Hocine...I had the 6 and the 7 but not the 14...Who would've guessed...But I'm gonna win this goddamn race...for sure! Don't believe me? Too bad for you 'cause I'm gonna win it!''

That was the day he had learned about his future wife...He opened the letter from home, a photograph fell out and he quickly picked it up. He saw Fatiha. He handed the letter to a young French worker with whom he was on friendly terms.

"It's a letter from my brother. Can you read it to me?'' Lucien had taken the letter.

"I am writing you what father and mother asked me to write you. The whole family is well and sends their love. The weather here is good. It's almost summer and in a month we'll be able to go to the beach. All your friends send their love. Ali and Néfissa are getting big. They would like you to bring them some clothes from Paris when you come. In a few months I'll begin a training program at a factory which has just opened near the town. Our father says you are over thirty now, that he is getting old and your mother as well; they wish God to give them a grandchild who will carry the family name. Father says you must come home and get married. They have found you a wife who is serious, pretty, and from a very honest family. She has gone to school to become a seamstress. Her name is Fatiha. She is Kaddour Chabou's daughter. She is seventeen years old.''

"Well...what do you know...they don't waste time where you come from!''

Lucien looked at Hocine and laughed, which annoyed him.

"Your wife will get a gold necklace and a pair of bracelets.''

Lucien laughed.

"Listen old man, you just have to try your luck at the races! Go ask Albert for some hints!''

Hocine remembered that moment perfectly; he had stopped looking at Lucien.

"Our father says he has put part of the money you sent home aside. As for the rest, he says it will be worked out."

Hocine had taken the letter back and quickly stuffed it into his pocket and in that moment it was as if he was still repeating the same motion. Why had he given in? He looked at the masseur who showed no fatigue. Warmth of the bath. Well-being.

"You worked in France?"

"And how I worked in France! Five years! I worked in Lyon and then in Paris. I worked the construction sites at Bagnolet, and then I worked at Montrouge and after that Monsieur Azoulay found me a job in Chantilly taking care of the horses. 'Rachid,' he said, 'you were with the Algerian troops. You like horses'. . . It's true I like them. So I worked in the stables; I gave them oats, hay, I groomed them."

He stopped talking and massaging and broke out in laughter.

"Now I take care of men!"

Hocine broke out in laughter too.

"And you take good care of them! But you must be tired now. Massaging is hard work."

"Oh! I'm used to it, but after a good massage, I have to recover my strength for the next one, and you have to stay here, calm like you are, dream a bit. . . and believe me, an honest wife is God's greatest gift!"

He left Hocine with a smile and went into a quiet room next door. He lay back, stretched out his arms and closed his eyes for better concentration and to recover his strength more quickly. Hocine noticed the youthfulness of his body; he would like to keep his own up, but how? His life in Paris was not one which preserved youth in a body, more like one that wears it down. He stretched out, letting himself fall into the soft calm of the after-massage. All around him men were relaxing like he was; stretched out, their heads wrapped in towels and covered by their robes, they wandered with their thoughts, with their dreams; some discussed politics or business. One of them had his ear against a transistor radio. The room-waiter offered tea and coffee. Hocine took a tea. He felt good.

Fatiha, alone in her room, sat on a mattress covered with a brightly colored Aures cloth. She looked at the opened suitcase next to her filled with her wedding gifts; absent-mindedly she touched the linen, took a jewel and then put it back, looked at a gold necklace. A childhood memory was stirred by the reflection of light on the metal. The sun was shining through the leaves of the orange tree in colorful balls. She was laying under the orange tree with her friend Myriem.

"Look, the oranges are black!"
"The sun is blinding you, the oranges are red!"
"Black!"
"Red!"
"Black!"
"Liar! If you can't look at the sun then you're the liar!"
They laughed. The oranges were red, the oranges were black... appearances...

At that moment her mother came in with some women relatives, all smiling, gay and chatting. Then came the midwife whom all welcomed respectfully. She approached Fatiha who was looking down at the ground. Her mother took her hand tenderly.

"My little girl, my dear."
The midwife sat on her right and put an arm around her almost with affection.

"You're going to be a woman! They say your husband is very handsome..."

"My little girl, my dear..."
Fatiha looked at neither her mother nor the midwife; she waited nervously with her eyes lowered. The midwife's

hand went up the length of her thigh. Fatiha contracted, moved back.

"My dear, my little girl..."

"They say he has traveled a great deal...so he knows about life...That's good for a man...a woman can be happy with such a man!"

Fatiha, not fooled by the words, tensed herself even more. The midwife slid her hand between her legs, reached the lips and then went deeper. Fatiha jumped back violently. The midwife sat up nimbly and yelled a joyful youyou which was immediately taken up and amplified by the other women.

"My little girl, my dear..."

Houria laughed for joy with tears in her eyes. Her girl, her little Fatiha was a virgin. She had known it all along but it had to be publicly verified and proclaimed for the honor of the family. Fatiha kept looking down. Oh, how she hated what had just happened; she rejected this 'verification' with all her soul; it felt like an unbearable and unacceptable wound. She knew this was the custom...for centuries and centuries women have had to submit to it...but was that any reason to continue to submit today? She could have never imagined how much she would hate every moment up to the wedding; let's get it over with quickly...oh, let's get it over with quickly! Fatiha let herself be led out of the room by her mother and the other woman.

Fatiha was passed from hand to hand like a doll. She was dressed and made up, the women turning her back and forth and in all directions. Finally they all looked at her, admired her, laughed with pleasure, then gently and gaily, and without some affectation, took her to the mirror. Fatiha looked at her reflection. She could not recognize herself. She ran her fingers along the plucked eyebrows completely transforming her face; the women broke out in laughter and youyous of joy. Fatiha remained still before the mirror; the women waited for a smile but she did not smile.

She had not wished to appear before her husband for the first time adorned like this but rather the way she had been before all these endless preparations, even though she liked her dress. She found it beautiful; it was in order to make dresses like this one and many others that she had liked learning to be a seamstress. She recalled the day she had designed a dress from her imagination and how the girl next to her had laughed.

"There's no use in tiring yourself out like that! What do you think all this is for? It's to mend socks!"

She remembered her anger at that laugh. She slowly turned her eyes away, apparently uninterested in her reflection. The surprised women became silent. Was it bashfulness? Was it sadness? They avoided looking at Houria so as not to aggravate this strange moment. The young today... really... who can understand them?

Fatiha sat stiffly in her wedding dress and waited. Her mother entered, carrying a tray of henna, followed by the other women adorned in gold trimmed velvet and silver laced muslin of many hues, deep blue, green, pink and garnet red.

Magic, movement. A vivid kaleidoscope.

Putting on their wedding jewelry they looked at each other, admired each other, found fault with each other. Some of them had antique noble airs about them, like idols or tragic actors with enlarged and darkened eyes, with silver plates and chains, bracelets and silk scarves. They sat majestically on the cushions arranged around the large room; each covered with a fabric as sumptuous as the women's clothes. They smiled at Fatiha who responded with a timid acknowledgment. Houria rolled up the sleeves of her blue velvet dress and carefully applied the henna to her daughter's hands.

"My dear, you are more and more beautiful!"

Fatiha smiled at her mother and contemplated her hands while they were being dyed red. Houria was surprised at her daughter. Always so lively, talkative and gay. Now so silent! Why had she changed so much? She refused to let herself believe that Fatiha was simply unhappy. As soon as the thought made its way into her consciousness, she energetically pushed it back.

"You're just intimidated my pretty, my dear, my treasure. . . I was too, back then. . . but I was happy. . . so happy. . . but I didn't show it. . . She's so like me. . ."

And to convince herself:

"Are you happy, my pretty?"

Fatiha did not answer; she was still looking at her hands. For a moment she wished her husband would come and free her from all this quickly. The husband she had yet to meet and knew almost nothing about. . . The absence of even an idea of his face was intolerable. It was as if he didn't really exist. An intolerable absence, and the intolerable presence of everything demanded of her to become his wife. What was demanded of him to be her husband? She had no idea.

The presentation of the gifts began. A smiling woman placed a package on the big tray and extended a thousand good wishes; another offered money. Houria, still carefully applying the henna, announced the sum loudly, smiled and bowed while the women again yelled loud youyous. Fatiha just listened and watched. All the joy and excitement became more and more agonizing. She could no longer hold back her tears. Only an old cousin noticed. She came towards her; caressed her cheek with a sympathetic look, leaned over and whispered into her ear:

"You must smile at life, my angel, because if you

don't, life will shrivel up like an old sheepskin in the sun."

Fatiha laughed.

"So, you see. . . we laugh like that, over nothing. . . and everything becomes as pink as your dress! Believe me. . . you have to smile at life, my angel."

She gave Fatiha another pat on the cheek, then called all the young women over to give them henna which would promote their swift marriage. They ran over with outstretched hands and laughing, turned around, the center of their palms colored with the magic red.

Fatiha caught sight of Myriem who came quickly to her. They embraced and looked deeply at each other with affection. They didn't need words to understand each other. Myriem saw Fatiha's distress; she understood her desires and dreams and her refusal to accept her fate. But what could she say when things were done like this?. . . impossible to change.

Leila, a young cousin, began dancing to the sound of the darbouka and tambourine. Her hips wrapped in a red, yellow and gold scarf, her agile shoulders, the beauty of her movements, of her arms and hands, of her rhythm, her sensuality, simultaneously full and light, all of this enticed Fatiha and Myriem. Some of the young girls joined the dance. The women began clapping their hands to the beat. Myriem wanted to bring her friend into the dance, but Fatiha remained still, her hands and feet bound in cloth, a prisoner of tradition. Aïcha, not missing a thing, approached Myriem and vigorously pulled her towards the dancers. She wanted to stop this conspiring. Her intuitive sense told her that her daughter-in-law had to be shielded from these friends whose lives would go on for a while as unmarried young women, some as school girls. Fatiha saw Myriem, followed by her mother-in-law, turn and give her an impish smile.

Aïcha was a beautiful woman who did not look her fifty years. Agile in spite of her dimensions and often exuberant, she seemed energetic and dictatorial, proud of the power and authority vested in her within the limits of a woman's universe. Next to her, Houria seemed discrete, reserved, and she was just that. Affectionate, calm and gentle, undemanding and very devoted to others, she smoothed out more conflicts than she provoked. Her presence was serene. She spoke little, listened and rarely gave an opinion. She considered her own opinion of little importance, accustomed to following her husband and always smiling as if life had spared her worry.

Fatiha, after comparing the two women, so different from each other, wondered how she would be able to live without her mother and with that woman who was to be her mother-in-law. Why did she have to change homes? Why did women always have to go live with their husband's family? Why couldn't they choose? Why was it that her husband would not come and live with her family? She knew that if she had asked these questions she would be told to hush up. . . just crazy ideas. . . they get you nowhere, her mother would say. . . Everyone has their crazy ideas. . . she would have to silence her 'crazy ideas.' Be quiet. . . she had remained silent for days. What she wanted to say was not what was expected of her. It made her apprehensive. She sensed it would go on and on. . . for a long time. . . for a long time.

She recalled the day Myriem tried to comfort her:

"'Fatiha, are you in love with someone?''

"No, that's not it. . .''

"Then, why are you so sad?''

"Because I don't want to get married like this! I want to go on at school; I don't want to live like our mothers, stuck in the house. I want to work! Why do they decide everything for us like in the old days?''

Myriem could find no answer.

"You're lucky, you are.''

"Oh!. . . for how long? My mother spoke to me about

Haddad's son, the one who works in the Ministry of Agriculture. I wouldn't be surprised if. . ."

A young pregnant woman walked through the court-yard carrying a bucket of water and some washing.

"That's my sister-in-law. Don't you recognize her?"

Fatiha could not. In eight years of marriage she had had six children; four of them had died. She was always sad and Myriem could not understand what had happened between her and her brother.

"My brother is very hard on her. I don't know why. And she takes it all without a word. She's completely passive."

"I don't want to live like that!"

"But your husband lived in France, Fatiha, he can't be like my older brother! He's more old fashioned than my father! He won't accept the smallest change. If it were up to him I would've never gone to school!"

"No. . .I don't want to live like that!"

Madame Suissi, Fatiha's former sewing teacher, had just come in and brought Fatiha out of her reveries. She came towards her with a smile, gave her a kiss and handed to Houria the gift that Fatiha's wrapped hands could not take. They looked at each other and remembered. . . their opposition to this forced marriage; their efforts to stop it; their powerlessness to change anything at all. Madame Suissi knew Fatiha had decided to become a teacher like herself but never dared to say so. But she could have. She was angry with herself for not having been able to convince Fatiha's father. She knew she had deeply disappointed the pupil she loved dearly. Fatiha had been cheerful, lively and intelligent, sensitive and always interested, full of questions and enthusiasm. She was angry with herself. It was not the first time it had happened and unfortunately it would not be the last. At times she was able to win over the parents of her students and change their futures, but this was very rare. In this case she had not succeeded and since

24

she could only find words that avoided the issue, she simply said:

"How beautiful you are, Fatiha!"

Fatiha, choked up, holding back her tears, tried to smile and lowered her eyes. Yes, Madame Suissi had disappointed her, but she did not blame her. What she could do was very limited in the face of her family's determination! Houria quickly took Madame Suissi to the table in the same way Aïcha had taken Myriem, and with the same concern: to protect the young bride. She invited her to have some cake and drink whatever she wanted, leaving her with Myriem, who had just noticed her teacher.

When Houria looked at her daughter she saw she was alone, withdrawn, lost in the contemplation of her bound hands. She remembered the day her husband had pushed her to announce the good news; she could see her dear little girl slowly going through her morning routine, so nonchalant.

"Hurry up, dear, you're going to be late again! Hurry up . . ."

She would very much like to be able to say those words again this morning. . . Her daughter was being taken from her . . . She could see her in her blue kabyle dress, with her long flowing hair.

"But dear, you haven't done your hair yet?"

Fatiha's burst of laughter. . . that marvelous laugh of hers!

"Why are you looking at me like that this morning? What's the matter?"

"It's just. . . just. . . never mind. . . hurry up. . .."

She hadn't the nerve to tell her. Her father told her of the future marriage that night; Fatiha was still; she suddenly lost her color and broke into tears. Houria recalled Madame Suissi's visit to talk about Fatiha.

"Fatiha is such a good student. . . it would really be a shame to. . ."

"Marriage is a more important thing than school for a woman!"

"She's still so young; she has so many plans; she likes learning so much. . ."

"Marriage is more important. . ."

Her father was so self-confident, calm and preoccupied with order and tradition.

"Fatiha is very gifted, she. . ."

"Fatiha is getting married; a woman's place is in the home with her husband and her children; that's where she has to put these gifts, as you say, to work."

"But one doesn't prevent the other, Mr. Kaddour! Today everybody's work is needed, including women's. . ."

"No! No! Not when men are unemployed."

"But women working doesn't increase men's unemployment, Mr. Kaddour, to the contrary."

"You can't make me believe that!"

"It's the truth all the same. . . and what's more. . . now women want to learn, work, and choose their own husbands. . ."

"Then what was the use in winning our independence if we're just going to copy everything the Europeans do? No! All that's no good! I know about life, madame, I come from a peasant family and I've been working in hotels for a long time now. . . I know about life. . . we want our daughter to be happy."

Houria had been silent throughout but each and every word of the conversation was engraved in her memory; she would not dare give her opinion; as a general rule what the father did was right. . . but why force Fatiha now? Why not wait a while longer? There was no rush.

Houria and Madame Suissi were reliving the same scene. Madame Suissi could not get it out of her mind; she thought of how powerless she had been to communicate with Mr. Kaddour; he agreed so naturally with his own decisions, so self-confident because he based himself on respect for the family order established for centuries for the good of all. Nothing she could have said would have broken through his convictions or have changed his mind. Then what would make him change his mind? Time? Probably... but how much time? She realized that as long as the Kaddours of this world could not be made to change their minds and accept that women could be trusted in modern social life the same way they had been trusted in family life, the same way they were trusted in the hard times of war, women's lot would only change with great difficulty. In order to alleviate some of the pessimism of her conclusions, she began thinking that maybe Fatiha's husband would understand her, be free from the prejudices paralyzing women's legitimate aspirations... why not?

The atmosphere grew more and more lively, the excitement rose; the dancers, more and more numerous, were seized by the rhythm. Houria decided it was time to unwrap Fatiha's hands and feet. This was done quickly. The henna was perfect.

Houria looked at her daughter with such tenderness that for an instant Fatiha felt happier; she felt like dancing and let herself be led by a cousin; her eyes caught the attentive look of Yamina, her young sister-in-law, and she smiled at her. Yamina responded with an affectionate wave of her hand. They were attracted to each other; they would be sisters; they would like each other...

While Yamina watched her young sister-in-law dance, one of Aïcha's cousins eyed her. She found her absolutely charming and ready to be promised to a husband.

"Your daughter is pretty, Aïcha!"

Aïcha smiled with pride; it was true... Yamina had a nice face and a good character which was better yet!

"My sister has a son..."

"She's still young, but we'd better start thinking about it! We have to marry our daughters while they're young, like in the old days! It's the wiser thing to do these days!"

"I was promised when I was ten...and with God as my judge...I have never regretted it...."

Yamina watched the dancers. How could she possibly guess that her mother and a cousin were deciding her future? Being of a docile and obedient nature, she did not suffer from her mother's authoritarian character; she admired her and tried to imitate her in all the household chores; she knew how to do these things very well...

Houria contemplated her daughter, who at last seemed to be happy, letting herself be swept up by the joy of dancing. These kids! What's going through their heads? Their sadness...like a cloud...like a very small cloud...that's youth...and that's the way it should be! Houria took a deep breath. Fatiha was happy. Thank you God! Thank you!

Fatiha danced with a liveliness unleashed by her anxiety, her worry, her regrets; she danced to forget and for the moment she felt free.

As for the men, they had just finished the marriage feast; some were talking, others singing, playing the tambourine or the darbouka. Someone started the dance of the scarves while two others mimed a belly dance, three young men imitated the women's youyous. Old women cleared the table silently and discreetly; the men paid no attention to them. Here, the men were among themselves, spoke among themselves, had fun among themselves. Hocine smoked and watched the dancers, as if he were watching a show, as if it were one of his friend's weddings.

"Hocine, you're a lucky man!"

Salah, one of his friends, called to him. He just smiled but did not answer.

"I would sure like to get married! But I can't...I don't have the money, I haven't worked for months...."

"Today's a holiday, my brother...so don't think about

it! Hocine's the one getting married..."

"In a year...maybe."

"In a year...yeah...seeing as you want it so badly!"

The three men smiled. Getting married. Have a wife and then children...Hocine would have gladly exchanged his future for that of his friend, but if he said so, Salah would think he was joking. It was not the first time Hocine had realized that you could not always speak the truth; he remained silent. A woman brought in a tray of henna with four candles. She turned ceremoniously towards Hocine, smiled and put two of his fingers in the dye.

"May this henna bring you happiness!"

May this henna bring you happiness! May this henna bring you happiness! The men's fingers reached out with the same magic phrase repeated time and time again. Then, in accordance with tradition, all the men dropped money into a big scarf on the floor. So many times had he dropped his offering for a friend getting married in Paris.

Paris...He recalled his arrival the first time...standing there holding his small suitcase, bewildered and surprised, hesitant, overwhelmed, he was both assailed and attracted by this new world. And today, after all those years of emigration, he still had those contradictory impressions. Assailed. Attracted.

The highway into the city had seemed immense. Then the river of cars, then the Goutte d'Or...the Maghrebian ghetto...His father did not want him to go back. Go back. Stay...

His father, surrounded by friends and family, smoking and talking, was completely satisfied with this traditional wedding. The traditions that he strove to maintain in everything and against all challenges, as it must be in everything and against all if one does not want everything to drift away, cave in and disintegrate. A son obeying his father and both of them obeying tradition; the social and ancestral edifice is consolidated. Most of the men talking to

Amor believed as he did. They had that proud air and calm self-assurance of those who are convinced they have acted correctly.

The taxis stopped in front of the groom's house; neighbors assembled at the door, laughing and talking, awaiting the groom. Amor, in a white gandoura and burnouse, almost regal, appeared at the doorway. Slowly, he advanced towards his daughter-in-law who had just got out of the taxi, her mother seemed to efface herself behind her. She lowered her eyes. Amor opened his burnouse and with a broad gesture, spread it over Fatiha's frightened and trembling shoulders. They walked at the same slow pace towards the house. An old veiled woman sprinkled orange flower water from a silver cup over Fatiha, then over her mother, then over the guests. The neighbors grew silent as they watched. Amor, like a high priest, performed all of his duties according to the tradition he was so attached to. Fatiha entered her new home under the protection of her new family patriarch; she had not dared raise her eyes to him; she entered under the protection of God, under the protection of the rites. But far from reassuring or calming her, these rituals worried, constrained and distressed her. She crossed the courtyard with eyes lowered; she did not see the carpets hung on the wall, on the clothesline, to greet her. She saw the rich, warm ones on the ground. Outside, the women let out loud youyous.

Led into her bride's room, Fatiha allowed the women to undress her while on the men's side, the party continued.

Mohamed danced, encouraged by the stares, singing and handclapping. In his exuberance he took off his vest and threw it to the onlookers. Salah, just barely catching it, broke out laughing.

"I didn't know Mohamed could dance like that!"

"Our dear Hadj Mohamed, always ready to show his

admiration and enthusiasm," exclaimed Salah.

The others stopped dancing to watch him and to encourage him to throw himself more ardently into the dance. Then they began dancing again, alone and together at the same time. Hocine looked on; it had been a long time since he had felt any desire to dance.

The final wedding night preparations were underway on the women's side. The women put the finishing touches on Fatiha's makeup. Aïcha placed a specially made charm around her neck, to bring her peace and happiness. Houria, contemplating her daughter, was deeply moved. A young boy was brought before Fatiha as a good omen. May the young bride have many children! Many beautiful children! And many boys! A good posterity is the greatest of blessings! Exhausted, Fatiha seemed indifferent towards everything happening around her. They could not have drained her spirit any better if they had intended to. . .; her mind was blank, dazed to the point of fainting. The women began singing a very soft song. The unrestrained noise of the party had now given way to waiting for the final stage in the marriage ritual.

Amor got up slowly, crossed the room and left the men's side. Hocine followed him with his eyes, once again feeling a certain admiration for his father. He admired the man fulfilling his duty to the end, with calm self-confidence. He felt so deeply different from his father. He was neither calm nor self-confident. He had never exercised authority. He shared in none of his father's convictions, none of his beliefs, even though he now acted as if he were in complete agreement. . . as if. . . In France he had grown used to acting as if. . . to acting as if he were not too lonely, as if he were not looked down upon at work, as if he were happy. . . Hocine knew his father had gone to warn the women, to tell them that it was getting late, that the time had come for the married couple to meet. He felt no desire

to meet his wife; at that moment he felt his lack of desire to
be an inexplicable flaw. He wished it were otherwise.

The singing stopped as Amor entered the bride's room.
He bowed his head slightly and touched his right hand to
his heart. He looked at his wife and said:
"It's time to make way for our son."
"Already," Aïcha said.
"You talk so much you can't see the time pass!" He
laughed.
"It's time my sisters!"
Amor left.
Fatiha quivered and took refuge in her mother's arms,
hoping to hold her back. Houria kissed her.
"My little girl, my dear. . ."
Aïcha took a last look at her daughter-in-law. She was
satisfied. Her son's wife was adorned just the way she
should be. She led Houria out. Fatiha remained alone,
standing in the middle of the suddenly empty room, empty
of voices, song, and laughter. She slowly walked to the bed
and sat down. She waited, immobile, worried. My dear. . .
my dear. . . her mother's whispers. . . Do everything your
husband wishes! Do not displease him, my angel! You are
going to be a woman now! If you do not want your husband
to dominate you, put your foot on top of his as soon as he
lays against you. She looked at the gold plated bronze hand
of Fatma hanging on the wall.

In accordance with the tradition, Hocine put a white
burnouse over his suit. His head covered, his face barely
visible, accompanied by his two friends, Salah and Mohamed, he traveled down the same hallway his father had
majestically walked down only a few seconds before. He
was smoking. Salah took out a bottle of whiskey and offered some to Hocine. Hocine hesitated and then drank
quickly. The hall was dark; the lights had been turned off;

one or two doors off the hall were ajar. Women's eyes. Quickly closing doors. To the surprise of his two friends, Hocine turned towards the inside courtyard. He paced back and forth nervously. Motionless and silent, they waited a few feet away.

The clear, open night sky; among the stars, the moving light of a far off plane. Hocine abruptly threw down his cigarette, crushing it with his foot and walked to where Fatiha, his wife, was waiting. His two friends gave him a friendly pat on the shoulder. The women, who had been hiding in the other rooms waiting for this moment, came out and yelled strident youyous the moment Hocine crossed the threshold. His two friends waited outside the door as if they were standing guard duty.

Hocine stopped for a moment in the doorway and looked at his wife. Fatiha got up abruptly; glanced at the man who had just entered, her husband, then lowered her eyes; she had barely seen him; only his gaze.

Hocine took off his bournouse and approached her with an awkward, nervous slowness. On the other side of the door guarded by Salah and Mohamed, the music, singing and youyous doubled in intensity; the excitement of the group grew; the women were waiting impatiently for the consummation of the deflowering ritual. On the men's side of the house the anticipation was less visible, but it stirred up the desires and imagination, and their memories of pleasure of the heart and body.

Hocine took Fatiha in his arms; she withdrew so violently that he sat down, took the teapot from a low table and filling a first cup, then a second, handed one to her. Fatiha took it, thanked him but did not drink. Hocine drank his tea gravely, hoping to overcome his anxiety. He was intimidated by this very young girl; she did not appeal to him; her body was not open to love, but he had to make a woman of her and quickly, since they were waiting outside.

But the more he thought about what he had to do, the more irritated he became at finding himself in this situation and the less he wanted to take Fatiha, his wife, by force. But it will be necessary to take her by force; she knows nothing of sexual desire and she is not open to it; she doesn't desire him and he doesn't desire her, yet he must make love with her, and quickly, because outside, people are waiting.

Fatiha moistened her lips and then put down her cup as if to obey her husband; she sat on the edge of the bed; Hocine closed the window and the outside noise died down. He began slowly undressing her. Trembling and without looking up she let him do it. You must obey your husband...do everything he wishes...But if you do not want him to dominate you... Remembering her mother's advice, the only advice she had been given, she awkwardly attempted to put her foot on Hocine's; the only thing she could do to defend herself against this stranger, her husband, who was already caressing and kissing her, holding her tighter and tighter against him. She felt the body of a man against her own for the first time. She tried to get away; she stiffened, struggled, closed up, attempted to escape. Hocine held her ever more firmly, both irritated and suddenly strangely excited by her resistance.

"Fatiha, don't be frightened, you're my wife..."

Fatiha tried again to escape from this man's heavy body, from this man's hard sex already penetrating her, tearing her. She screamed and moaned under the assault. A sharp pain within and the horrible sensation of powerlessness.

The ears glued to the door outside heard the young woman's cries. The youyous fused, echoing each other, repeated and amplified.

On the men's side a few good riflemen fired the wedding volley.

The joy was at its zenith, the party reached paroxysm.

Fatiha cried. She felt something like hate for the first time in her life. Hocine hesitated to take off her blood-stained nightgown which was expected outside. He took it off gently, though irritated by her crying. He covered her with the sheet. She burrowed under it and for a few seconds Hocine pitied this very young woman, his wife, dainty, pretty, attractive but too closed to be seductive. She was not the woman he would have liked to live with had he been free to choose. Had he known her when he was around twenty . . . maybe . . . but today . . .

He left quickly and threw the blood-stained nightgown to the women. Ancestral gesture. Blood sacrifice? The women caught it in the air. The youyous broke out like brass bands. They waved the nightgown over their heads and began dancing.

Hocine, hugged and congratulated by the friends around him, had only one desire, to get out, to get out quickly. Mohamed and Salah had been waiting behind the door, their bodies stiffened with desire, and then, relieved by that strange and secret complicity of men, proud of their virility and in that moment deeply bound together. They laughed.

"What if we go drink to this?"

"Let's go out, we can get a drink somewhere; there must be a car available."

It was as if they had read Hocine's mind.

On the women's side the deflowering dance continued, becoming frantic and a bit savage. The rapid rhythm and some of the more piercing, louder and more gutteral, youyous, seemed to be calling back moments from the past.

Yamina sat in a corner watching the scene, disturbed;

she was disgusted by the blood-stained nightgown; she could not bear any more and ran out.

The rhythm intensified even more; the excitement mounted; body and soul are seized by the songs and shrieks emanating from the depth of their being. . .

Amor, massaging his moustache, something he did every time he was either sad or very perplexed, watched his son leave. At that moment he was proud and full of gratitude towards his son, but especially towards God. Well done, my son! Well done! The family is consolidated and I will not die without grandchildren. May God be praised! He offered cigarettes to the other men around him and smoked calmly, happy. Fatiha's father, sitting next to him, felt the same satisfaction. For a few seconds he thought of his own wedding with emotion, he had been so overwrought he had remained impotent for a dreadful moment while the impatience on the other side of the door increased. He smiled at his recollection. Then he recalled that great day, that happy day, when he and Amor had finally decided on the marriage of their children:

"Aïcha chose well for our son."

"Our daughter is uncomplicated, a good girl, and bright; we have never had any problems with her; the money we asked you for was only to buy what the children needed; in our time we could have had a prince's wedding with all that money. But today everything is so expensive. We are just simple ordinary people, but a wedding is a wedding and our children must start out on the right foot in life.

"It was a lot of money for me; but a father has to be happy to see his son married before he dies; I have been looking forward to this day impatiently!"

"A marriage is a serious thing; your son waited and he was right. Like my father used to say, your marriage should be remembered for a hundred years!"

The men had laughed, while Fatiha, not suspecting that her father had just decided her adult life, served them coffee, then had softly and discreetly withdrawn, oblivious to everything that had just happened.

"Your son has traveled; he will be a good husband for our daughter."

"It's high time he came back and lived with us! It's not a bad thing to leave home but you have to come back. Your daughter is beautiful and you have brought her up well; she'll know how to keep him here!"

They had concluded the marriage. Everything had gone as they had planned; the children had obeyed, and today, as they savored their coffee, they also savored the happiness of being sure of having accomplished what had to be done. This was one of those beautiful moments in life when you are in complete harmony with yourself, with all animate and inanimate things, moments that are as warm and comforting as the sun.

Fatiha put her wedding gown back on and sat at the edge of the unmade bed, her face contracted, she seemed neither to see nor hear; she felt that vertigo from within like you have the day after a very high fever. The blood-stained nightgown was spread out at the foot of the bed; she looked at it a second, then turned her eyes away holding back with all her might the impulse to vomit. The women were noisy as they usually are on these occasions. Houria kissed her daughter affectionately, lifted the nightgown as if it were a valuable object and looked at it with admiration. You see, my daughter was a virgin! She did not dishonor us! Aïcha was satisfied and tapped her daughter-in-law's cheek. Her son's wife was just the way she ought to be, reserved and simple. They had chosen well. May God be praised!

Fatiha, immobile, allowed herself to be hugged and, because she had to, smiled at all these women congratulating her and wishing a thousand best wishes.

"May you live a long and happy life!"

"May God grant you beautiful children!"

"Be happy, my pretty!"

"Why are you so pale?"

"It's nothing," Aïcha said quickly. "She's fine! It's just the joy!"

She and the other women laughed. A few mischievous looks of sexual complicity.

Fatiha had a very strong desire to get out, to run away and be alone; but she was tied down by a thousand invisible fetters that seemed indestructible to her. In her mind she relived this recent jumble of events and the feeling of being tied up, restrained, became so intense she felt ill. A cry rose in her throat and choked her. She felt like she was being squeezed very hard; she gasped for air.

"You don't feel well, my dear? My dear. . ."

She grabbed her mother's arm violently.

"My dear, my dear. . ."

A woman energetically sprinkled the young bride's face with fresh water. Ah! These kids. . .How fragile they are! They've been too coddled. . .and now! In our day. . .

To get out. To be alone.

The time for separation had come, and Houria, upset at having to leave, encouragingly caressed her daughter.

"We'll come back and see you, my dear. You'll be just fine here in your new home. Now you're a woman! Yamina will be your friend. You're lucky to have such a nice sister-in-law."

She controlled her emotions with great difficulty and spoke to try to overcome her tears. Fatiha was crying. Kaddour pulled his wife away with an affectionate sweep of the arm.

"Come on, come on, you aren't both going to cry! This is a great day! You'd think we were leaving for the moon!"

He laughed. Aïcha was showing a bit of impatience; she was cross and irritated by her daughter-in-law's sadness, how uncourageous! She wanted to cut the scene short; she approached Fatiha and tapped her on the cheek.

"Come on, come on. Now you're a woman; you have to be more energetic!"

"Take good care of her," Houria whispered as she left.

The men shook hands, acknowledged each other with their right hands over their hearts and then embraced at length. Fatiha remained motionless as if she were shackled.

Houria stopped just outside the door and forced Kaddour to listen to her:

"Our baby doesn't look happy; she didn't eat, didn't smile; she's crying. . .what if we've made a mistake. . ."

"What are you saying woman! It's not easy to leave your parents; she was happy with us; but a time comes for everything. That's life. She has to get used to it! She's a woman now. We have made her happy so you have to laugh and not cry!"

"Oh!. . .Laugh!. . .The face can laugh. . .the heart knows the wound it bears!"

"Come on, come on. . ."

Kaddour led his wife away.

"We'll come back and see her often."

"No, woman, not as long as she's not used to her new family; we would only do her more harm than good."

Back in the bedroom, Aïcha was stroking the hair of her son's wife, straightened a lock, looked at her, and then led her away by the hand.

"I'm going to introduce you to the men of the family; you must bring honor to your husband! You have to smile!"

The men were drinking coffee; Yamina was serving; she saw Fatiha enter with her mother, smiled and left with the tray, like the perfect little mistress of the house. Hocine was there with his father and uncles. Allaoua, his younger brother, was talking with some cousins and neighbors. The men, smoking and laughing, looked up as the two came in:

39

Amor's and Hocine's eyes lingered on Fatiha an instant and then turned away. Aïcha presented her son's wife to each member of the family.

"Bachim, allow me to present Fatiha, my eldest son's wife."

"May God bless her!"

Presentations and blessings followed one another like litanies.

Fatiha let herself be embraced by the men of the family. None of them looked at her for any period of time except Allaoua, whose eyes followed his young sister-in-law with a certain insistence and daring. Fatiha met his frank, direct and friendly look and then turned to her husband. He wasn't looking at her.

Fatiha was alone in her room, waiting for her husband, as Aïcha had asked her to do. A disagreeable, ambiguous wait. She did not want to see him come in; those moments the night before had been so odious...yet something within her longed to know more about him.

They were now husband and wife for life. Fatiha was unable to comprehend her life at present, nor imagine what it would be like tomorrow, or the day after tomorrow... but one thing was for sure: she did not want to be unhappy; she believed in happiness; she wanted it to be possible and refused to think that her husband would not take her aspirations into consideration and understand her need for a life different from that of his mother. She stretched out on the bed, her arms down the side of her body, along this body which now had such a completely different presence to her, something indefinable since all the pre-marriage preparations, since last night; wounded yet present, infinitely present. She looked about her, trying to familiarize herself with the room, her room, their room, her new universe. A tapestry she would not have chosen hung on the wall, clashing colors, reds, greens... Turkish women bathing in the countryside... with dead stares. She would ask her husband to take it down. On the floor next to the bed there were two sheepskin rugs, a stand with a large white brass tray. Nothing in this room was hers. Not even the things neatly arranged in the light-colored wood wardrobe which had been given her by Hocine's family. She had not yet adopted them as her own, and adopting them is what counted. She was not in the mood to adopt the things in this new house where she must live from now on.

The family was assembled in front of the television in the large living room next to their room. Fatiha heard a few shots from the cowboy movie and then the clear voice of her young brother-in-law, Allaoua, an aficionado of westerns and movies in general.

"We could have at least turned the TV on in time to see the whole film!"

"For what these American films are worth! Nothing but violence!" Amor said.

Ali, their little five-year-old brother, was also fascinated by the TV while sitting on his father's lap and picking his nose.

"Why did the sheriff die?"

Allaoua took the boy's fingers out of his nose and said with a laugh:

"It wasn't the sheriff, it was a bandit, dumb donkey!"

"I'm not a dumb donkey!"

Fatiha smiled. Ali reminded her of her own little brother; she quickly pushed the family memory out of her mind; she thought of Hocine. How would they be able to live together without love? Without friendship? How would they be able to simply talk to each other? Who was he? What did he want out of life? Would they have to stay here, with his parents, always? In other places, and also sometimes here, people married for love. They had a life ahead of them to be shaped together. In other places, and sometimes here, there were independent women who could do whatever they felt like doing. . . She began reflecting on ways to influence her fate; none of them excluded Hocine.

The film ended without surprise. The good guys won and the bad guys were killed on the main street of a western town. The man and woman, who loved each other, triumphed over all obstacles to live their love. They gave each other a long kiss.

Amor, who had no liking for these long kisses offered for public contemplation, said disgruntledly:

"They shouldn't show films like that in our country!"

He was happy that the good guys beat the bad guys just the same; it satisfied his justice-infatuated soul; it was the love stories he didn't like. While stroking the silk-soft curly hair of this beloved son he said:

"These stories make our youth stray away from our way of life!"

Aïcha agreed, delighted. If she had her way they would not watch such films; at least that's what she proclaimed.

Allaoua was amused; he knew his father would criticize the program endlessly but enjoyed his evening in front of the TV nonetheless; and as for his mother, he suspected her of being quite interested in the scenes of other places in spite of what she said.

The announcer was now giving some news on the agricultural reform. Aïcha took away the tea tray.

"That's all for tonight. It's time to go to bed."

"That's a beautiful village," Amor said still watching the TV images.

"But I wonder how happy the peasants are in these new villages? If my father was still alive would he like them...those cooperatives? He was so independent! Those houses are one on top of the other!"

Allaoua looked at his father and then back at the TV.

"They've got water and electricity in those houses. That's good in itself!"

"It's good but it's not enough; they're one on top of the other, my son, you can't do anything without the neighbors knowing about it; you have to protect your privacy; you're still too young to understand; you'll see when you get older."

"We live one on top of the other in the cities; and here, only a stone's throw from Algiers, we're not far from our neighbors..."

"And we're getting more and more individualist! How do you figure that?"

"The peasants in Aïn El Bordj said they were happy and that they were prospering; all the same it's better than being exploited by a boss and being at his mercy, isn't it?

"For sure; but our cousin in Boukalfa doesn't seem so satisfied! My son, you have to know why men are satisfied and why they aren't satisfied. It's not enough just to say they are satisfied, or not satisfied. Some aren't satisfied when they can no longer steal from others; others aren't because they aren't free to choose their job; others because they don't have one...it's not the same thing at all."

"Papa, where's the sheriff?"

"My son, he's gone to bed; even sheriffs sleep, you know!"

He laughed and kissed the child who was looking at him with the greatest of trust, and then got up and took him to bed.

Aïcha passed Allaoua in the hall.

"Have you seen your brother?"

"Papa took him to bed."

"I don't mean Ali, I mean Hocine."

"He's not in his room?"

"No."

"Then he must be out!"

"Insolent! Aren't you ashamed to answer your mother in that way!"

Aïcha left outraged, cursing these kids who have absolutely no respect. Allaoua smiled and quickly disappeared. He loved his mother very much but took pleasure in making her grumpy, he loved to contest and tease her. She went into the living room where her husband was listening to the radio and smoking. She hesitated a moment, then came over to him.

"Your son has not come home! Isn't he ashamed to leave his wife like that!!. . . You men, you allow yourselves such liberties. . . I thought my oldest son would be different!"

Amor looked at her calmly and smiled:

"Come on, it's not late. He hasn't seen his friends for so long; they've got things to talk about; anyway he knows what he has to do."

He looked at his watch, smoking and listening to the radio, half asleep. Aïcha sat down and began sewing, irritated. From time to time she looked at the clock and sighed. Tired and wanting to cut short his wife's familiar sighs and comments, Amor got up and turned off the radio.

"I'm going to bed."

Aïcha pretended not to hear, determined to stay there sewing until Hocine came home. Oh. . . she would not say anything. . . but she would look at him and he would understand what her look meant. . .

Amor, guessing her intentions, turned around:

"Come on, let's go!"

Aïcha hestitated, then half-heartedly put her sewing away and got up with a sigh.

In the bedroom Fatiha had fallen asleep completely dressed and was curled up on one side. She was dreaming.

She was in the street in her wedding gown, walking. There was an intense blurred light. Birds flew out of the fig trees. A woman in a blood-stained nightgown walked towards her. Fatiha recoiled from her own apparition. Hocine, dressed in a blood-stained burnouse, came towards her but passed without seeing her. Enormous faces assailed her. The sounds of the party were deafening. Silence. An oppressive silence. Fatiha walked on; her dress was violently torn away from her. She screamed and woke up with a start, her throat was dry. She was frightened and looked all about her; she didn't know where she was, just like a child awakening from a nightmare. She curled up, hugging a cushion against her breast, struggling with the still present images of her dream.

Hocine and his friends were sitting at a table in a bar full of men. They were drinking beer. The strong, deep, magnificent voice of Oum Kalsoum was coming from the radio; the voice captivated and mesmerized Hocine and his friends, who had talked a lot, drank a lot and now became silent.

Men, alone, in front of their cup of coffee or their glass of beer, they seemed not to hear, not to see anything. Salah, preoccupied with his favorite subject of the day—work in France, earning money, saving, being able to get married—started the conversation again and spoke directly to Hocine.

"So, is there still work in France?"

"Less, you know a lot of our brothers are forced to come back."

"Yeah, but they say there is still work the French don't want to do. . ."

"Yes, jackhammering the streets. . . collecting garbage. . ."

"What do you do in Paris?"

"I work in a construction site."

45

"My cousin drives a bulldozer. Before that, he drove a crane; he makes good money."

Hocine ordered more beer.

"Not everybody makes good money. Everything is very expensive in France, especially nowadays! And housing... you have no idea what it could be like: shacks, workers' tenements, ghettos...and it's not cheap! France is no paradise, don't kid yourself! I have a friend in Barbès, he lives in a room that's only ten square meters with five other workers. Can you imagine that?"

His friends looked at him, surprised because his tone had become vehement, and because he usually spoke so little.

"And what's more, you can do the best you can, you can break your back at work, you can be polite and there's always some guy gonna let you know you don't belong, that you'd be better off somewhere else, that they don't want to see your face, and because of the unemployment, even those who said nothing before will insult you now, just as soon as look at you...thàt's the way it is!"

He drank his beer. His friends studied him closely.

"So why go? Why do you stay there?"

"My man, you have to earn a living someplace!"

"I wouldn't go play slave in France!"

Mohamed spoke with anger. Hocine was surprised.

"Here or someplace else, my man...what's the difference?"

Well, it's not the same."

Hocine gave him a friendly pat on the back.

"When you're in our situation you're always a slave to something...that's the way it is! How long've you been looking for work?"

"Over four months."

"You see, you're a slave of unemployment, I think that's the worst of all because they convince you that it's your fault, that you don't know how to work, that you're lazy, that you're a wimp... The work we do in France...I don't wish it on you...but unemployment is even worse..."

"I want to stay here in my country and work here. My father used to say that exile was the brother of death. The brother of death. It was true 'til the very end for him, he died over there."

The three friends fell silent for a moment, saddened by the death in exile of Mohamed's father, who had been forced to leave his country just so he wouldn't die of hunger!

"We're not alone, my man...all the poor in the world are potential emigrants...and all that shouldn't be, but it is!"

"I thought it was easier here to find work...it seems to me it could get better? Maybe we have to take a bit more initiative...but that's impossible."

"What prevents us from doing it?"

"Are you kidding me? We're not the ones who can start the machine rolling. You know as well as I do that if you don't know someone to get you work or papers, you don't get anything. If you know someone in a good position, well, then it's all right, otherwise you're up a creek; each man for himself and hustling makes it! Nothing you can do about it, my man. That's the way it is!"

"It's colonization that made us get used to it. That's what's sickening!"

"Maybe...but that's the past, colonization...it's all over now, you gotta wake up! And you know, over there in France, they weren't colonized, and hustling is what makes it there too...that's human nature...and that's what goes on in Russia and in China too...you gotta change it...but I don't know how..."

"I think you're exaggerating a bit," Salah said. He appeared shaken, angry, thoughtful. "Our country has changed a lot since independence. We've got factories, we extract oil for ourselves; the peasants live better since the reform; my brother, this is a growing country; that's it. . . a growing country! You can't have everything at once."

Hocine broke out in laughter.

"You talk like they do on TV or in the papers. My man, life is not TV, not the papers!"

"What about the women in Paris?" Salah asked seriously. He decided to drop the conversation about work in France for the moment, ready to take it up again when Hocine was less negative and better disposed to inform him. He had made up his mind; he would go to France and make enough money to finally be able to get married; because it was no life remaining single, without a wife, without children. . .no, it was not a man's life!

Hocine, slightly drunk, patted Salah on the shoulder and laughed.

"Ah, women! Are you dreaming again? Don't believe it, it's not easy to have fun either."

"You can't make me believe that."

"You'd rather believe those who tell you stories? My brother, you musn't dream like that, you musn't dream like that. . .I dreamed too. . .but the truth is. . ."

"You're married now; you could care less!"

Hocine did not respond. Oh, yeah, he was married. . . and what he had been forcing out of his mind with all his might came back, Fatiha's face, her crying, their wedding night. He ordered a beer.

The waiter was confronting a drunken client at the bar.

"No, I told you I'm not serving any more."

The stubborn client leaned on the counter to get better balance.

"Come on, just one, just one and I'll go, I promise!"

"We're closing. Are you deaf or what?"

The waiter called the manager. The drunk became irritated, hit the bar with his empty glass and yelled:

"This isn't a Mosque here!"

This provoked laughter from the other drinkers and from Hocine and his friends.

"That's it, we told you," the manager said, taking the man by the arm to put him out. "I don't want any trouble with the cops."

And when the man resisted:

"If you think it's too early, go complain to the government; I'm not the one who writes the laws; do you want them to close my bar? Is that what you want?"

"I want a beer. . .I don't want them to close your bar. . .I want a beer! Just one! God damn it, Kader, I swear I won't go if I don't get another beer! I've been coming here for a year. . ."

"And even if it were ten years it would still be the same. That's it."

The manager forcefully took the drunken man to the door; he tried unsuccessfully to get loose; he remained outside the closed door cursing the manager. "It's the police and the government who prevent honest citizens from drinking a beer when they're thirsty." The manager cocked his head back and laughed.

"He got like that in France. . . O.K. brothers, we're closing for today. See you tomorrow if God wishes!"

He lowered the lights and the customers left. The drunken man staggered up the street.

"Going home?" Salah asked. He wanted to stay with his friends.

The customers dispersed and the three friends remained in front of the door, undecided.

"It's such a nice night," Salah insisted.

"Is everything closed now?" Hocine asked.

"Well, yeah, my man, it ain't Paris here!"

"Why don't we go to the beach?"

It was Hocine's idea, which surprised Mohamed. If he had a wife he would go home. This Hocine was incomprehensible. They headed for the Pine Club beach.

Mohamed wanted to tell Hocine that he did not understand him but he didn't dare.

"Are you going back to France?"

"I don't know."

They walked on silently. The air had sobered them a bit. Salah made Hocine look him in the eyes.

"Tell me, Hocine, what you said in the café, was it because you were drunk?"

Hocine smiled, looked at the sea, at the horizon, threw his half-smoked cigarette in the sand and stepped on it.

"My brother, it's better to tell the truth; better the truth that hurts than a lie that feels good. I told you the truth."

"I want to go to France all the same. If I come to Paris will you help me?"

"Of course, my brother, of course we'll help you; but don't get your hopes too high!"

"If I don't I'll never have enough money to get married."

"Don't get married!"

"You got married, didn't you?"

"What, me? I was never in a hurry; and I only got married to obey my parents' will."

"But aren't you happy?"

"You know, my man, a piece of advice, that's one question you should never ask yourself, it complicates everything. . . We're alive. Some days are good, some days are bad! That's life. . ."

The three men sat down on the sand and fell silent. Mohamed watched the sea rise and fall, suddenly he yelled loudly:

"I don't want to live like that!"

"What makes you think I want to live like that?"

Mohamed, surprised by Hocine's answer, looked at him, then looked the other way.

Salah thought:

"Well, what sort of life did you want?"

But the question never made its way to his lips. Had he asked it, what could Hocine have answered? Perhaps only: "I don't know...I don't know...things happen...I don't really decide. Maybe that's what destiny is all about... luck..."

What if luck and will were one and the same, and sometimes the bad will of others? At that moment he felt good on the deserted beach in the clear night; he thought it a beautiful beach, maybe the most beautiful in the region and that being able to walk around there and swim could change one's life... The song of the sea that evening resembled Oum Kalsoum's song.

Late that night Hocine finally got home. Fatiha was asleep, curled up fully dressed. Hocine watched her briefly.

"Fatiha!"

She woke up with a start, sat up on the bed, saw Hocine and looked at him strangely.

"Why didn't you go to bed?"

"I was waiting for you; I fell asleep without realizing it."

Hocine turned off the main light, switched on the night lamp and undressed. Fatiha slipped under the sheets drowsily. Hocine stretched out alongside her, remained motionless for a while, then took Fatiha in his arms. He still smelled of alcohol, and the smell surprised and offended her. He held her against him very tightly; she tried to get loose from his hold. He made her open herself, made her receive him. His desire was sudden and violent. Fatiha's sore sex, assaulted once again, suffered the hard wounding penis yet another time. She yelled out; Hocine's lips smothered her cry; he held her under him and he was overwhelmed by love's rhythm; he felt pleasure as the orgasm quickly came. The whole body in ecstasy; that inexplicable magic; and that marvelous relief; he withdrew, relaxed, lit a cigarette, smoked it slowly, and then fell asleep.

Fatiha remained awake; she dared not move for fear of waking him; she was assailed by thoughts, impressions and that searing in her sex, the throbs of pain. Is that what the night of a husband and wife is? The thought that Hocine had been drinking frightened her, because in her family alcohol meant unhappiness and almost certain downfall. With an infinite sensation of loneliness reaching vertigo, the bed suddenly seemed to pitch like a boat on the sea. She clutched the sheets. She smothered a cry, burying her head in the pillow; then the tears came, releasing the tension.

II.

Hocine and his father walked to the Mosque side by side.

"My son, I know you come with me today to make me happy; this is good but it would be better if you came to pray."

Hocine did not answer, he looked at the street full of people; children were running back and forth, the shoemaker patching shoes like in the old days, the men waiting at the barber's, a television repairman seemed to be trying to convince a client that his TV could not be repaired, something the client obstinately refused to admit. The TV repairman had not existed when he was a boy but the barber, butcher and cobbler had been there, in the exact same place. Women were shopping and all those people seemed to have nothing better to do than to walk up and down the street to buy or to talk. That villa was owned by a rich colonizer before. He had left; the wash dried in the windows; children yelling and playing came out from every door; the facade had not been kept up very well, there was even a crack that needed repairing; the flowers grew freely all over; it was all marvelous! It was so full of life. Not prosperous enough, but so alive. At that moment Hocine's town completely seduced him again.

"My son, did you forget your religion in France?"

"I don't know father, I don't know what I forgot."

"I am going to pray for you and for your wife, for your future family. May God give us a little grandson! I'm getting old, my son, I'm getting old!"

Hocine turned towards his father. He was full of vigor, upright, young in spite of a few wrinkles and some white hair.

"You don't look it!"

Amor smiled with satisfaction; he took pleasure out of feeling in good health. . . and. . . virile! But he quickly chased those thoughts from his head as they were now approaching the Mosque.

Inside a lot of men were already praying fervently in low voices which filled the space and enveloped them. Hocine carried out the rites but his thoughts were elsewhere. The colors attracted him; the pink and green of the columns: the reds, blues, and yellows of the tapestries and ceramics; he had always been attracted by colors. Ah!. . . build a house of mosaics! His eyes followed the arabesque; his mind wandered. Paris. . . Paris, the big foreign city where you could break away from tradition, where you could remain anonymous. Paris, the big dazzling city that devours you, entices you, so full of men from all over, so amazingly diverse, and yet a place where you can feel so lonely. Paris, the only place where, from time to time, he had felt that captivating impression of being free, which he had never felt to such a degree anywhere else.

The faces of the men praying were replaced by those of Arab workers, workers like himself, living in the same hotel, in the same neighborhood, walking in the streets, drinking a coffee at the corner bar. That man over there with his head lowered reminded him of a worker whom he had never seen smile. Today he was there with his father but it had been so long since a prayer had last come to his lips. It had happened naturally; he felt no emptiness, no need, no sadness. Among these men, praying out of habit or deep belief, he felt no frustration, no impatience. He was far from being preocuppied with God; it was man that preoccupied him, and life; whenever he asked himself why people are the way they are, good and bad, just and unjust, gentle and violent, he never went as far as God. He would stay within the world of man where there were so many questions and so few answers . . .

The prayers of the assembled men became more intense.

Hocine fell into daydreaming which haphazardly confused images of his childhood, images of his youth, of his marriage, of Fatiha, of the women he had met or dated, of his life in France. Strangely enough a sentence came to his mind, over and over again:

"I don't know what I have forgotten, father."

He was surprised. Then the thought of the shish kabobs his mother made so well came to mind, spiced just right, roasted, sweet smelling . . . On the way home they would buy some lamb and figs, which his mother loved. How did these men manage to pray so long? Hey, isn't that Si Lakhdar over there? Was he praying or just pretending? He was too selfish to waste so much time praying!

Hocine, aware of being distracted, imagined Si Lakhdar just as distracted by his business and bargains . . . A master hustler that one is! He knew how to profit from any situation without ever dirtying his own hands . . . It's an art!

His father, having finished his sincere dialogue with God, headed for the exit, followed by Hocine. They entered the street which was lively, full of people and the good smell of grilled lamb, sauces and mint. Beggars were asking for alms from passersby who were distracted or already preoccupied with business or shopping. An old man called upon God and held out a practiced hand. Hocine thought he had an ascetic face. How had he fallen that far down? Who begs in Paris? Human beings destroyed by life and alcohol, gypsies with their babies in their arms, the youth they call 'marginals'. . . and here? Old people, especially old people, some of whom had the look of old prophets, women hiding their faces behind faded veils, and sometimes children too. Hocine felt mixed sentiments of pity, irritation and worry like he did every time he saw this.

A man was taking pictures with an old camera he had found in the garbage and had jerryrigged. Hocine stopped and looked at him. You can take pictures with that? The photographer thought Hocine wanted his services and then insulted him under his breath when Hocine walked on.

Tape recorders! Don't you want a tape recorder? Radios. Brand new cameras?

"There are too many peddlers, my son, too many peddlers! Young people want everything they see; that's not good, that is not good!"

Hocine laughed.

"When there's not enough work to go around, you try to get by as best you can. In Paris a lot of our brothers are reduced to that. . ."

"Peddling in the streets, no, my son! There are already too many peddlers, too many peddlers . . . and how do you know it's not all stolen goods?"

Hocine laughed again.

"Hustling! Some say it's not exactly stealing! But it comes from all over. . . from here and elsewhere! My father, there's not enough work, look at all these young people in the middle of the week, coming and going. . . it's a godsend when they find something to sell. . ."

"The country is old, my son; but it's like a child in all the fields of this modern life that have shaken the world;

we aren't 'developed' enough as they say—what an expression!—for all these young people to have work. . . .That's the way it is!''

"I haven't found any either."

"I know, my son, I know; but you will; you'll find a good job that will give you enough to raise your family without shame."

"Maybe."

The two men continued to weave in and out through the street peddlers, the shopkeepers, the strollers and the buyers. An old man sitting against a wall with a bucket of chickpeas between his legs reminded Hocine of a friend at work in Paris; he looked so much like him that he could have been his father. An amazing resemblance! A very young man followed Hocine, convinced he would sell him the jacket he was touting as the most marvelous there was. He turned away, disappointed. I swear they all must be broke! A jacket like this. . .at a quarter of its price!

"There are too many peddlers in the streets, my son, too many peddlers in the streets. . .it's not good!''

When Hocine and his father arrived back home with their arms full of packages, Aïcha welcomed them with joy and the menu was immediately, completely transformed, and enthusiastically so. Later the men were served in the yard under the shade of the fig tree. Hocine and Amor relished the shish kabobs admirably prepared by Aïcha. She reached the peak of her happiness when Hocine told her that no restaurant, no matter how many stars it had, served such good shish kabob. She hugged him and returned to the kitchen, convinced that her oldest son was the worthiest of maternal love of any son there ever was. She wondered if Fatiha was really the woman who deserved such a son! After the men had eaten, the women ate their meal. Fatiha, who was used to a common household life, could not adjust to the traditional ways of life respected in her new family.

Hocine, her husband, remained a stranger, a stranger she had to serve by day and who had every right by night. She refused to believe that such an unforeseen and profoundly unacceptable situation could last; she looked for ways to change it, but hadn't found any. She had the impression of constantly pounding on an unbreakable wall. She was going through discomforts she had never been through before; at times she felt like weights were on her breast, and sometimes in the middle of eating she couldn't swallow another bite. Boredom, loneliness, the impossibility of speaking out, the drastic break from everything that was her happy life before the marriage, left her lost; she would often have to hold back tears that came on so spontaneously that it amazed her.

Fatiha, her sleeves rolled up, was sloshing water in the courtyard; she vigorously scrubbed the cement floor with a straw broom. She worked quickly, with a vengeance, as if the work would appease her loneliness, her disappointment, her homesickness, the sadness and the wounds of body and heart. Aïcha watched her with satisfaction from the doorstoop. She realized that Fatiha adapted with difficulty; but it was not important; it would pass; she was a hard worker and that was the essential thing. Ah, yes. . . that was the essential thing! A hard working young woman and the home was saved. Then she turned back to the kitchen, reassured.

Hocine came back home. Fatiha, absorbed in her work, did not hear him. He went to the bedroom, opened the door and called her. She straightened with a start and saw him motion her to come and join him. She looked at him in surprise, hesitated, and since he insisted, lay the broom against the wall, washed her hands at the courtyard faucet, then walked towards their room.

Aïcha, having vaguely heard Hocine's voice, appeared

once again at the door looking around the courtyard for Fatiha, and saw the abandoned broom and bucket.

"Fatiha!"

Fatiha did not answer. She went to the couple's window, listened for a few seconds, heard them, frowned, and put the broom and bucket away still grumbling. Making love in the middle of the day! Preventing his wife from working! No, that's not good! She did not agree at all with her eldest son! But no sooner thought than forgotten. She had so much love for him, so much understanding; he had been alone in Paris; he had no work here...Come on now...he's going to make us a sor! God be praised! She smiled with happiness.

As for Allaoua; he was enjoying the complete freedom of youth. He was at the beach with Ahmed, who was a year older, and Karim, who was a year younger than he was. Whenever Ahmed was around you could be sure the conversation would get around to women, sex, and his real or imaginary adventures; he was in full flush discovering his desires, needs, and troubling emotions, and all the obstacles and forbidden things that govern the relations between men and women.

"A woman told me I was a champion for my age!"

"A champion of what?" Karim asked Ahmed, who broke out in laughter putting his hand on his sex.

"A champion of that, Hadj Karim!"

Karim, embarrassed and disconcerted, took a stone and threw it as far as he could but did not reach the sea. He knew at that moment that Ahmed looked upon him condescendingly and he hated it.

"Have you already made love?" Ahmed asked him provokingly.

"Love...love to a woman?"

"Of course idiot, not with a goat!"

Ahmed pushed Karim over in the sand with ease since

he was much stronger. He took great pleasure in doing it.

"Did you hear that, Allaoua? Karim is a virgin!"

Allaoua laughed so as not to be suspected of this blemish which he shared with Karim.

"I don't know where to find a woman to do those things."

Ahmed laughed all the more and Karim, more and more ashamed of his inexperience, vexed and irritated with being treated in this way, ready to fight Ahmed, wanted to run to the sea but did not dare.

"I can find as many as you want! Right, Allaoua?"

Allaoua acknowledged without conviction.

"Fifteen days ago I met a young German girl," Ahmed continued; "we did it in the rocks; she gave me a wrist watch!"

Ahmed reached in the pocket of his vest laying on the sand and pulled out a wrist watch. Karim looked at it with admiration. He moved closer to Ahmed in order to get a better look and Ahmed made a sudden move of grabbing Karim's sex. Karim jumped back violently; his desire to fight became more violent. . .but Ahmed always got the upper hand, so what was the point?

"You got a pair or don't you?"

The eternal masculine challenge. . .Karim got up and went to urinate a few steps away.

"That's it. . .use your hands!"

Allaoua thought Ahmed was going too far but he was too torn by his own desires, and got a sort of pleasure from these verbal excitements. Karim came back and stood still before a rock.

"Look, a lizard!"

Ahmed picked up a rock and wanted to throw it at the little animal bathing in the sun, but Allaoua stopped his arm.

"Why do that? It's alive!"

Karim walked away muttering. "He's right Ali, when

he says they're all obsessed. . . and what's more, I would've refused the watch! It's all a little sickening. . ."

"Come on back. Don't go away. . ."

That was the way it always happened. Ahmed pushed Karim to the limit. Karim, who was too weak to fight, would then leave and Ahmed would call him back. Ahmed needed him, needed his weakness to prove his own strength; he need to prove himself. Allaoua would not have admitted to Ahmed for all the money in the world that he had never made love. His brother's recent marriage, Fatiha's presence, exacerbated his desires and dreams. Make love. . . make love. . . Desire as hot as the sun; expectation that was simultaneously anxious, painful, and exciting; uneasy and feeling good; and the looks of women that draw the body taut as a rope. That explosive enjoyment of sex!

Fatiha and Yamina were cleaning house like they did every day. Yamina was humming; she enjoyed her young sister-in-law's presence very much. They smiled and helped each other in the never-ending household tasks. Sweep, dust the furniture, carefully clean the copper in the living room, shake the carpets, put things away, stock up on water, wash and prepare the meals in the cool kitchen, roll the semolina while squatting under the fig tree in the courtyard, peel the vegetables Amor brought every day from the market on his way from work. Meanwhile, Aïcha arranged the semolina and makrouds in the living room cupboards always ready in advance, along with the red peppers, chocolates, and spices, all of which was under her vigilant control. The linen was stored on the upper shelves. In this way it absorbed smells a perfumist could never hope to match. Aïcha was truly the high priestess of the great cupboard! She always kept the key on her belt with the house keys. This surprised Fatiha, as the living room cupboards in her family never deserved this excess of honor nor this surveillance! In the beginning she was amused, but now it irritated her. Allaoua, every chance he got, carried out an underhanded but methodical war against this organization, which he never missed a chance to call archaic. He did not like the idea of linen being mixed in with the food—young people's ideas!—and did not appreciate that that cupboard was locked. He teased his mother about it every chance he got. Aïcha paid no attention; her parents had done things this way, her grandparents had, and that was the way it had to be, so why would it be wrong today?

In spite of all these household chores, Yamina and Fatiha managed to amuse themselves like children from time to time. They would laugh for no apparent reason, or when the little ones would do something silly or start running after the birds only to stop with their noses in the air, flabbergasted by their rapid and precise takeoff.

"Why they got wings and not me?"

They broke out in laughter. Ali wanted an answer and not laughing; so he would sometimes get angry and run to his mother's skirt. His mother would defend him without examining the facts. "What have they done this time to my little treasure, to my darling? What have they done to my little man?"

"Yes, why have they got wings and not us?" Fatiha wondered.

She liked the two little ones very much but Aïcha would hardly permit anyone to spirit them away from her. She wanted to be the center of affection and she wanted everything to pass through her first. She would then generously redistribute according to the merit of the moment.

Aïcha observed the affectionate collusion between Yamina and Fatiha without much enjoyment, since she had also noticed a lack of it between Hocine and his wife. Aïcha could not really understand her young daughter-in-law's character or behavior. She asked herself questions which turned and turned in her mind without ever finding an answer. Fatiha eluded her completely. She seemed to be a stranger there, as if she were visiting, submissive, polite, the guest who knew she would soon be leaving. No sign ever expressed a joyous acceptance of her new life; no statement ever came forth that indicated projects for a common future. No dialogue with Hocine, no look, no tenderness witnessed the birth of the love that life required. Nonetheless... this was where her home was, this was where she had to live with Hocine, my son, her husband with their children... because the house is big enough for us all. Aïcha wanted to talk about all this with her son, but she did not dare. He went out a lot; he was looking for work without success. May God grant he find something quickly! My dear son, we have given you a wife, you must give us a grandson! Are you happy, my son?

That day Yamina and Fatiha were preparing an ousbane couscous. Yamina, squatting, scraped the tripes in an enamel basin under the faucet. Fatiha chopped the vegetables and was having fun with her sister-in-law while she was peeling onions which made her cry and had driven the little ones away.

"Look, Yamina, if you want to be an excellent cook you have to do things in the right order, like my mother always said! Otherwise it will be spoiled! You start with the garlic, then the onion, then the spinach stems, forget about the leaves; after that you mix it with harissa and throw a fistful of raw rice in the mixture; here, help me stuff the tripe; do you see how clean it is? Come on, let's go, stuff, stuff!"

They broke into laughter just as Aïcha came into the kitchen.

"Come, Yamina, come, I have something else for you to do; Fatiha can finish by herself."

Yamina regretfully obeyed her mother while Fatiha,

who understood clearly that her mother-in-law did not like to see them together, having fun and not knowing what it was all about, continued her work without showing the least reaction. This only irritated Aïcha more, as she hated this attitude of indifference that she saw as a bit devious. She had been separating them so much lately that it could only have been intentional. Fatiha went on working as if nothing had happened. Dusting, putting things away, washing, ironing, cooking; all these things passed the time which strangely did not really seem to be her own any more. The feeling of something temporary and, at times, the certainty that the future would be different from the present (because this was not what she expected from life), clashed against its opposite: the feeling of immutability, powerlessness to change things at all, the sensation of impassable obstacles, of walls.

Aïcha was seated in the courtyard, sewing. Hocine came home. She held her arms out to him. He came to her and she made him sit under the fig tree. She looked at him with such love it was impossible to resist her; the sun wasn't any warmer than her eyes!

"My son, your father has gone to City Hall. Come, my son, sit down. . . do you want some coffee?"

"Yes, thank you."

Aïcha turned and called Fatiha.

"Fatiha, my daughter, make us a coffee."

The mother and son remained silently next to each other under the fig tree. Then, no longer able to hold it back, she asked him the question that had been plaguing her for days.

"My son, are you happy?"

Hocine smiled.

"A wife is the reflection of her husband, my son; if you are happy, she is happy."

Hocine said nothing and Aïcha dared not break the

worrisome silence.

Fatiha served the coffee and went back to the kitchen.

The following day, Malika, the younger sister of one of Aïcha's childhood friends, arrived from her home town. Malika had a beautiful, open, gay and smiling face; she was lively, dynamic, seductive like her elder sister whom Aïcha had so dearly loved and still loved. They had so much news to exchange, so many things to say.

"I was so sorry that I wasn't able to come to your son's wedding. Fazia was even more upset. I'm told you chose well, that your daughter-in-law has been to school..."

"School! The main thing is that she knows how to cook and clean! There are too many girls getting married today that don't know how to make a couscous!"

The two women laughed.

"Times are changing, Aïcha; the young can't be like us! Everything is changing in the village too."

"Women are women and men are men! And that doesn't change!"

They laughed again.

"I'm going to tell you something...I don't think Fatiha looks well; I wonder if..."

"What? Already?..."

"What a hurry you're in!"

"And your daughter-in-law?"

"Oh, her, she doesn't know how to do anything!"

"You're exaggerating, aren't you?"

"No, unfortunately, I'm not exaggerating!"

"And your son?"

"I don't see him any more; she monopolizes him completely. That's one thing she knows how to do."

"Your daughter-in-law isn't stupid; that's how we keep our men, that way and in bed."

Aïcha pointed to her stomach and the two laughed just like they used to back in the village.

"The young say that we are men's slaves and they don't want to be that way any more; but the men are also *our* slaves."

They laughed even louder. Allaoua came into the courtyard and Malika looked him over from head to toe.

"Allaoua! How you have grown! You're a man now!"

Allaoua kissed Malika and then walked away slowly. Aïcha watched him with admiration.

"What a handsome boy! Have you found him a wife?"

"Not yet; and it won't be easy! He doesn't want to do anything like the others; he stands up to everybody, even his father! He told us he wouldn't get married like Hocine, that he wants to know his wife and he wants her to know him; that they want to choose and love each other."

"I know all about that! At any rate, Hocine, your eldest, is married; it was about time; you're going to have a beautiful grandson, a beautiful boy this year."

"There's something that bothers me about my son's wife: she doesn't talk; she looks sad."

Malika tilted her head.

"It's true, you'll see; I don't understand her; I don't know if they're happy; I would like Hocine to stay here with us so much. I wished and prayed that he would come back and get married to one of our women here; I was so afraid he would get married in France; I don't want him to go back; I don't want him to."

Malika saw and shared the agony of her friend; her own eldest son had gone to work in Germany and had not come back; they say that he lived with a German woman over there! Ah, she preferred not to think about it, or talk about it!

"He won't go back; he won't leave her here alone, come on. . . stop worrying; worrying only makes you old and you know we don't have the right to get old anymore!"

Again the two friends laughed.

"Malika, my friend, you are young! Won't you stay

with us for a few days? I am so happy you're here; but what are these medical tests you were talking about? Are they really necessary? I really don't like that! In the old days we took care of ourselves without all that and we were no worse off! And we didn't die any more than now.''

Malika laughed.

''I don't intend to die!''

''That's not what I meant to say...''

They embraced each other.

''We women have always got some problem...but it won't be serious; you look good...I would even say you're getting younger...''

Aïcha was worried. She took her friend by the arm and led her to the house; she cursed life for being so fertile in unanswered questions, in illnesses that came without warning, in these medical tests that had to be done...in marriages that were no longer what they used to be, in sons that want to break with tradition...She gave a long sigh that Malika fortunately did not hear because the little ones ran into her arms yelling.

Amor, Hocine and Allaoua had been served dinner and then the women ate in the evening coolness of the courtyard. Malika did justice to the chekhchoukha Aïcha had prepared for her. Yamina was coming and going from the kitchen to the courtyard, carrying water and cookies. Then she sat down next to Fatiha whom, from time to time, Malika discreetly watched while telling Aïcha everything that had happened in the village: marriages, births, illnesses, disputes, reconciliations and deaths. Fatiha was not listening; she could hear the noise from the forbidden street covered by the sound of a foreign song from the record shop next door. She would have liked so much to have been able to go by herself, choose a record that she liked, discover new ones; but this was denied her. While she spoke, Malika, a shrewd psychologist, foresaw all the problems her friend would have with her young daughter-in-law. She was obviously miles away in thought, unsatisfied and so spiritless. Even though Fatiha had participated with pleasure in preparing the dinner, when it came to enjoying it, she was no longer hungry.

Lying next to Fatiha, Hocine finished his cigarette and put it out in the ashtray. He turned to her and wanted to kiss her. She pushed him away and abruptly rolled over. He backed away, jarred, nervous.

In the living room next to their bedroom there was a soccer match on television. They could hear the yelling and snatches of the enthusiastic comments. Hocine felt like getting dressed and watching the match. Fatiha tried to catch his eye; she wanted to talk to him, to clear the air, to tell him what she felt, to tell him she was not happy, that she did not believe she would have the strength to live like this, without the freedom to go out, as she had before their marriage; to tell him. . . Hocine was irritated and tense. He abruptly turned, took her in his arms and forced her once again to make love.

The children's room was like a little nest full of human warmth. Allaoua and Ali slept on two juxtaposed mattresses, Yamina and Néfissa slept side by side at the other end of the room and tonight Malika slept in the middle of the room. The regular breathing of the children could be heard. Malika was not asleep. She was kept awake by her worries; she feared they would keep her in the hospital under observation; she felt like running away before she got there; and what were they going to find? She chased the thoughts from her mind and allowed her recent memories to come back. Aïcha and her daughter-in-law, charming but too 'foreign'. . . as if she came from somewhere else. . .

Allaoua was not asleep; he was kept awake by desire; he was aware of the opulent, attractive and warm woman;

he remembered Malika's eyes, her admiring eyes, her smile, her mouth; he glanced at the little ones sleeping; he listened to Yamina's breathing; she was calm.

Aïcha and Amor had just woken each other up in their room. Aïcha gave a great sigh.

"But wife, why are you sighing like that? You turn and turn, you woke me up!"

"I'm worried about Malika, they're going to give her tests at the hospital..."

"She looks perfectly healthy...it certainly can't be very serious..."

"Oh, nothing's ever very serious with you...and what about Fatiha? Haven't you noticed anything?"

"Like what?"

"Don't you see she never speaks, you never get to know what she's thinking...our son has married a mute and you find it normal!"

"It's not that bad! It's better to speak too little than too much! And he's not so talkative either; they suit each other!"

"And what if we were mistaken about her? What if our son is not happy?"

She sighed and Amor, annoyed, turned his back to her.

"Let's go to sleep, ok?"

Aïcha stopped talking and tried not to sigh any more; she was used to not being understood when she was worried and to having to think by herself until she had lost the meaning of the thoughts she was harping on or until she was so upset with the emotions generated that she would feel sick.

Hocine dressed and left the room without saying a word. Fatiha, cradling her head on her knees, was crying; she was listening to her sorrow, her disappointment, her loneliness.

Hocine walked around the courtyard, lit a cigarette and blew the smoke towards the sky; now that he was smoking two to three packs a day he could rarely smell anything; but at that moment a light breeze blew the smoke away and because all of his senses were excited he smelled the heavy odors of the Algerian earth; the smell brought on fleeting images of the past; but tonight that past held no charm for him. He questioned it, it underscored his extreme loneliness, his sense of uprootedness, his anguish and his ineptitude to love. He was fleeing the memory of the stunned look on Fatiha's face; he was fleeing her expectations which he was aware of but rejected because he was afraid he would be unable to meet them; because he only knew how to be quiet when the gap separating him from the other seemed irreparable What could he say to Fatiha? He had lived so many moments she knew nothing about and she would never know anything about; moments she would not be able to understand. How could you communicate to the other what you have lived, why you did it, if ever you knew . . . and what it did to you? He had suffered loneliness so bitterly that he convinced himself it had now become the expression of his life. He could have accepted a presence that was all love, complete devotion, but not some new questioning, sensitivity, not this young girl he saw full of secret grievances, most of which were probably subconscious; not this body that would not give when he desired it. He walked back and forth in the courtyard and felt the strong desire to go back to France. Not because he was better off there but because the problems were now more familiar than those he had to confront here; over there his loneliness was sort of normal and never intruded upon; he could drown himself in it until it became relaxing and sometimes until he blanked it all out.

While Hocine was persuading himself that he should go back to France, Amor and Aïcha were making love with all their body and soul, so deeply accustomed to each other, so irremediably united, so peacefully linked for better and for worse that their sexuality was still very much alive after so many years of living together and in spite of the inevitable shocks of life. Their sexuality had the richness of a great irrepressible call, always renewed and so much more powerful and simple than the will of man.

At the same time, Allaoua, running from a real dialogue with Fatiha, could resist his desire no longer. He got up, led by his desire like a sleepwalker. Taking a thousand and one precautions he tiptoed, stopping to listen to the children's breathing, reassured by the regular rhythm, then approached the mattress where Malika lay. She was awake and turned quickly, guessing his intentions. In her sudden movement one of her shoulders became exposed. Allaoua knelt and lay on her, carressing her shoulder and face, kissed her, took her breast in his hands. Oh, the marvelous breasts, soft and heavy!

"Allaoua! My God! What are you doing? Go back to bed immediately!"

She tried to speak as low as possible. Allaoua put a hand over her lips and continued to kiss her. Malika pushed him with all her might but silently so as not to wake the children and create a scandal. Allaoua clutched her, his head in the hollow of her opulent breasts, in the hollow of a woman's generous splendor.

"Allaoua, I beg you!"

Allaoua, mad with desire, held her so tightly she could not break away. The woman was soft, round, hot. His sex, searching that of the woman's, found it, humid, open, deep, marvelous.

Malika decided to leave.

"But, my sister, you were going to spend several days with us!"

"Yes, but I had a dream . . . I forgot to tell you I was supposed to visit my husband's family and my dream told me it would be better if I went right away."

"But what about your medical exams?"

"There's a hospital there too."

"If you wait a little, Hocine will come back and take you to the station."

"That's not necessary, my friend, you know how well I know the way and my suitcase is not heavy."

Malika kissed her friend affectionately. Aïcha was so surprised by the sudden departure she did not know what to say. She was hiding something from her, but what? Had she offended Malika? Or had someone else? But she did not seem to be angry. What of this dream? What the devil did she dream?

Just then Allaoua came in. He backed off slightly, looked at Malika, lowered his eyes, then looked at his mother.

"Malika is leaving us earlier than planned. Walk her to the station, will you?"

"No, my sister, don't bother anyone please. If my suitcase were heavy I would say yes, but it's light. God bless you! God bless you all!"

Again she kissed Aïcha very affectionately and left.

Aïcha watched her leave and whispered:

"It can't be because of the dream she's leaving so fast? What happened?"

Allaoua leaned against the fig tree.

"What? She had a dream? It must have been a nightmare!" He laughed.

"Insolent! You have no respect! Oh la la la!"

Aïcha turned towards him furiously.

She went back in, lamenting. While the yelling children ran across the courtyard after their mother, Allaoua sat against the fig tree. He grabbed one of the passing children. It was Néfissa, in tears.

"He took my ball!"

"Then take it back!"

Néfissa broke loose and screamed even louder. Allaoua watched them and smiled; then he thought of Malika; she had left because of him; she had not said anything. Thank you Malika! If she had stayed, would he have gone to her again like the night before? When he thought about those crazy and marvelous moments—which is what he had been doing all day and which had caused a few blunders at work—what predominated was that deep satisfaction of finally having known a woman; it was this magnificent revelation of his own body and that of a woman's; it was the memory of that paroxysmal desire which he had obeyed; that force followed by that appeasement. In spite of it all he had few regrets. The retrospective fear of a scandal fortunately avoided did not carry much weight. Nevertheless he was a bit ashamed to have given into his desire and to have constrained Malika to submit. It went against all the theories he defended with such conviction. But was it his fault he couldn't make love to a woman who also wanted him without that deciding his whole future in the process? He was too young for his future to be decided but not too young to desire this self-fulfillment. This pleasure, this joy. Incapable of getting down to work, of reading, or staying in the house, Allaoua went out to look for one of his friends.

Fatiha had just finished washing the floor. The radio was broadcasting a chess lesson to which she paid no attention. She stopped housecleaning, sat on the mattress, lay back a minute, sat back up, looked at her fingernails, turned the radio dial. Static; then the singing of Warda El Djazairia blared out and became clear. Magnificent. Fatiha listened, hummed, imitated the singer, made fun of herself and danced a few steps. Hocine came in; he saw Fatiha in the middle of the room, the housecleaning stuff spread around; he turned off the radio.

"Put on your veil, we're going to buy you some shoes.

My mother told me that you need some shoes."

Fatiha was surprised and looked at him without moving.

"Well, what are you waiting for? Why are you looking at me like that? Don't you know me yet?"

"Why a veil? I've never worn a veil!"

"You're a married woman now; you know how attached to modesty my parents are!"

"So what? I won't wear a veil!"

"You'll wear one or we won't go out."

"Then we won't go out."

Hocine looked at Fatiha, stupefied by this new resistance, his authority wounded.

"We will go out and you will wear your veil! What is it you're looking for? To get insulted by the men and even the kids? Do you want me to be ridiculed? I'm telling you, starting today you will go out with your veil or you won't go out at all!"

Fatiha stared back at Hocine. Two forces were sizing each other up. Finally she looked aside; she took off her apron and took the veil her mother-in-law had left for her in the wardrobe. The veil she had sworn would remain there. She put it on her face slowly; she wrapped herself in a cloak. She had apparently given in but he had not breached her resistance. Hocine watched her put it on, reassured. She had given in. But this clash had left them more nervous, more irritated with one another.

In the street walking one step behind Hocine, Fatiha, hurt from having given in, was happy to be out of the house just the same. Even if she had a veil she was happy to be in the street, to see people, stores, to be out of the house, and for the first time she felt the desire to provoke Hocine. For an instant she considered ripping off the veil and walking behind him with an exposed face. What would he do? What would he say?

Something within her wanted to express itself and she

was conscious of it. She felt like running but she had to walk; she felt like ripping off her veil but she had to keep it on. She felt like. She had to. She felt like. She had to.

Once they had arrived at the shoe store Hocine had chosen, he entered first, followed by Fatiha. A young woman dressed European style, a woman of her age, without a veil and apparently alone, was trying on shoes at will. Fatiha looked at her.

"What shoes do you want to try? Hurry up; we aren't going to spend hours here; I hate the shoe stores here, or anywhere else for that matter!"

"Why didn't we go to Algiers? With my mother we . . ."

"And why not Paris? There aren't enough shoes here? What shoes do you want to try?"

Fatiha pointed to a pair of shoes the young woman had chosen, perhaps to oblige Hocine to notice her; but he had already noticed her; he quickly looked away.

"These appeal to me too."

She went out and looked at the window display followed by the salesman and studied the shoes for a while; Hocine was getting impatient which did not displease Fatiha.

"You are right, madame, you have to take your time to choose what you like and what suits you."

Fatiha tried on several pairs of shoes, contemplated her feet, listened to the advice of the salesman who, while attending to her, perceived not only her taste but mood, conflict, and sadness as well.

"I think I'll take this pair. What do you think, monsieur?"

"I think they suit you well; you have feet easy to fit . . ."

Fatiha enjoyed speaking to the salesman while ignoring her husband.

"Are you going to make up your mind, yes or no?"

"Yes, I'll take this pair."

Fatiha pretended not to have noticed Hocine's impatience, nor his irritation with the salesman he judged much too friendly. He paid and they left.

"Does that salesman amuse you?"

"Me? I was choosing a pair of shoes; if you didn't have the patience to let me choose you should have left me there by myself; did you see that young woman in the store by herself without a veil? Nobody was abusing her, nobody was insulting her! I used to go to stores by myself now and then and it was a real pleasure; with you it's . . ."

He stopped with a violent expression on his face.

"What do you mean?"

"With you . . ."

"With me?"

The tone of his voice was so violent that Fatiha preferred to be quiet. Hocine wanted to grab the package from Fatiha's hands and throw it in the middle of the street but contented himself with walking faster.

He was alarmed by this reawakening of his own violence, and to see that it was so close to the surface. It had been such a long time since he had felt these pulls; he thought they had left him, that he had become passive, indifferent to everything; he never fought any more; he let things be said; he let things pass . . . And now he felt it again with this young woman, his wife. And there it was, this marriage, rather than bringing peace, was a source of conflict, frustration, and of this resurgence of his violence. He did not want this violence. He did not want any conflicts.

Fatiha was not discontent with having provoked anger in Hocine; it was her subconscious response to the authority she had been suffering since the wedding; it was also because they had finally talked! It was not a dialogue but rather a confrontation, yet through the words and through this commonplace incident of no importance Fatiha had broken the silence which hurt her so badly; she had dared to

76

speak to him, to hold her own; he had gotten angry; she had touched his sore spot and with one stroke she felt not only stronger but closer to him as well. They were no longer strangers to each other.

That night Hocine felt like going for a walk with Fatiha along the river. The evening was so nice.

"Come on, put on your veil, we're going for a walk."

Fatiha was surprised by the proposal and the tone of his voice, which was more friendly than imperative. But she was just as irritated as she had been a few hours earlier with the 'put on your veil'...

"But it's dark out!"

"It's nice out, put on your veil."

"I have to wear the veil even at night?"

"Don't start again, will you!"

Fatiha slowly put on the veil, threw a scarf over her dress and followed Hocine out.

They walked in silence. Then Hocine took Fatiha's hand to help her walk in the dark and without hesitation she let herself be led. This hand which held hers tightly was something new and agreeable; it was as if they were going to walk a long time in the night until they became friends, until they became used to each other, until they desired to speak to each other, to embrace and to kiss, because he was a man and she was a woman, because they were both alone yet joined for life by marriage, because each of them wished for tenderness more than conflict. Hocine stopped quickly and Fatiha bumped into him. He lifted her veil, held her tightly and kissed her; he wanted to make love, there, on the ground, under the sky. Maybe it was the too insistent call of his body, so long deprived of a woman; perhaps it was the only way to reach Fatiha, his wife, at that moment. But she stiffened and resisted. He let her hand drop brutally and returned to the house. She had to run just to follow him. She had felt like staying there, immobile in the night and letting him go; but she followed Hocine and returned to the house, behind him.

Friday, day of rest and family festivities. The whole family of Aïcha and Amor walked toward the beach. The crowded bus had dropped them a few hundred meters away. The road was wide and beautiful with orange trees on both sides. Allaoua picked up a few fallen oranges which made his father indignant.

"But father, they were on the ground! They were going to rot."

"If everybody did that! And who would let oranges rot anyway? I'd like to know. If they were picked at the right time we would pay less!"

The little ones, indifferent to the controversy, grabbed the oranges like balls and went running with their new treasure. So Amor ignored the oranges "that should be picked at the right time and that we would pay less for"; he admired the large villas along the road, "villas of really high standing rented beyond a doubt to Europeans, civil servants in the embassies and others. . ."

Hocine walked beside his father secretly amused at his indignations. It had been a long time since he had been roused like that by things "that should be different than they were"; one would never cease being indignant. He was surprised by his father's extreme sensitivity next to which he felt infinitely blasé.

Aïcha and Fatiha were veiled and carrying baskets; the little ones ran towards the sea with shrill yells and still holding their oranges. Yamina, who was to look after them, ran behind; they were apt to run right into the water at that speed! Fatiha, while now walking with her mother-in-law, thought about the walks she used to go on with her parents along the beach. It seemed like such a long time ago but in reality was only yesterday! How she wished she were there with her brothers and sisters, whom she thought about so often, and with her cousins and friends. Everything had been an excuse for laughter and play. But in a few moments she would be able to swim. She liked swimming so much that she would be able to forget her past and her nostalgia. Just the same she did not feel the same burst of happiness but rather, she felt confused. It was as if even small pleasures were forbidden her.

As soon as they reached the beach Allaoua undressed and ran straight to the sea followed by the two little ones who adored imitating their big brother. Aïcha had difficulties walking in the sand; she did not really like these excursions. . . she was content to stay in her house, in her courtyard, under the fig tree; you lose your breath walking like that in the sun. . . but you have to make the children happy; Amor and Hocine quickly put up the tent. Aïcha lay the baskets on the sand and saw that everything was in order, nothing had spilled. Allaoua brought Ali back screaming. He had thrown his ball in the waves and was going to jump in fully dressed. He curled up in his mother's dress as usual; whatever the cause of his yelling and tears might be, his mother always managed to comfort him. Yamina brought Néfissa back by the hand. She was better behaved.

"Hey. . . you could've helped us put up the tent!"

Hocine was speaking to his younger brother. Allaoua laughed and ran back to the sea.

"Oh, these kids!" Amor sighed, happy to be at the beach.

He undressed quickly and lazily lay back on the hot sand. Aïcha did not appreciate her husband's ways and let her disapproval be known with a very noticeable pout.

"Come on, wife," Amor said when he saw what she was doing, "we're at the beach!"

Aïcha cocked her head back. She would certainly never become accustomed to these ways! She took out the thermos and offered coffee, and as Amor and Hocine eagerly accepted she asked Fatiha to take it to them. Fatiha handed the coffee to the two men basking in the warm sun.

Fatiha signaled to Yamina and they both went into the tent. They came out a few minutes later in bathing suits.

Aïcha choked on her coffee.

"Yamina, where did you get that bathing suit? That's no way to dress! You should be ashamed, both of you, to get naked like that! And in front of everybody!"

Fatiha broke out laughing.

"Naked? That's my spare bathing suit; it fits Yamina very well!" Hocine looked at his mother affectionately.

"Oh, listen, mother, everyone has bathing suits like that now at the seaside, look!"

"It's natural within the family," Amor said. He found the one-piece bathing suits completely decent and proper.

Hocine looked at his wife's childlike body, thin, almost fragile, then turned his eyes away.

"Fortunately," Aïcha muttered, "there are still women with self-respect!"

She pointed to a group of veiled women wetting their feet and laughing. Allaoua came back from the water wet and out of breath.

"The water is great! Mother, you should come in!"

The displeased Aïcha turned towards Amor.

"You should watch your son better! He is more and more insolent! It's his studies that make him like that. Maybe we should do like in the old days."

"Like in the old days, like in the old days, it's not like in the old days any more, mother!"

Allaoua laughed and planted a furtive kiss on his mother's cheek, wetting her with salt water; she wiped herself quickly, grumbling but happy. He ran back to the sea, inviting Yamina and the others to follow.

"I wonder what we'll do with Ali if things keep going this way."

"Wife, we still have time to think about it."

Her husband and Hocine laughed.

Fatiha and Yamina slowly walked towards the sea. Fatiha threw herself into the water with joy; she noticed that Yamina splashed about in the waves.

"I'll teach you how to swim!"

But Fatiha wanted only one thing at that moment; to swim, swim as far as possible. She swam with large strokes, free and happy at last.

Aïcha came to the water's edge, lifted her veil and wet her feet carefully. A man ran by in the break of the waves, spattering her by accident. She walked grumbling back to the tent, outraged.

"They really have the devil in them! It's terrible!"

Hocine had been tanning in the sun for a quarter of an hour before he saw Fatiha swimming far out to sea. He quickly ran into the water and swam in her direction. Fatiha could not hear him calling but when she looked towards the beach she saw Hocine waving her in. She swam back. As she approached Hocine and Allaoua, Allaoua splashed her, which was not appreciated by her husband.

"Can you go play your tricks somewhere else, Allaoua?"

"What's the matter?" Fatiha asked.

"Why were you going out so far?"

"I usually swim much farther and for a much longer time!"

"You've swam enough for now and you shouldn't go so far out to sea. Do you like having men follow you?"

"Having men follow me?"

"You didn't see that man swimming near you?"

"No, when I swim, I swim!"

All her happiness evaporated immediately; she swam back to shore with large strokes and did not pay the least bit of attention to Hocine. What's the matter with this family that they have to ruin everything like that! And her husband...even less tolerant than his father was! Arriving at the tent, she wrapped herself in a large beach towel without looking at Aïcha who had guessed what had happened and thought Hocine was perfectly right to have made her come back; she had swum enough...what if she was expecting...she could lose it!...

"You should get dressed, Fatiha, you'll catch cold. Hocine was right to tell you to come back."

"Right? Why?"

Fatiha, who was as irritated as she could get, answered with violence; she looked her mother-in-law up and down for a second and then looked out at the horizon. Hocine was swimming far out, free. Yamina, not knowing what Hocine had said, signaled to Fatiha. Allaoua surprised Yamina, making her fall. They laughed. Fatiha looked at them and then at the people on the beach playing like big kids.

Amor, tired out from his very short swim, called for a good piece of chicken. Aïcha offered him a thigh which he quickly devoured.

"Are you hungry, Fatiha?"

"No, thank you."

She no longer felt like swimming nor eating; she wished she could just leave; she lay back in the sun and pretended to sleep.

In the sea, far out, Hocine was swimming.

That night in their room... Aïcha seemed vexed and sighed as she went to bed.

"Why are you sighing like that, woman? We had a great day at the seaside; it was sunny; the children had lots of fun; they will sleep well!"

"I'm worried about our son. Fatiha and Hocine don't get along."

"What makes you say that?"

"Come on, it's obvious! You never see anything and you don't understand women!"

"Oh? I don't understand women? What about you, always making problems over nothing!"

"I don't want him to leave for France again, don't you see?"

"I don't want him to leave for France either."

"We have to know what's going on. You should talk to him."

"I'll talk to him. Now let's sleep."

"If only this woman knew how to make him stay, but they're like two strangers together; they don't get along!"

"Relax, she'll know how to make him stay; wait until a child comes." He laughed.

"That's just it! She should be pregnant; you know when a woman can't have any children..."

Amor laughed loudly.

"Aren't you in a bit of a hurry?"

And since Aïcha continued to sigh:

"Come on, stop worrying; no time has been lost. Hocine will have children like we had! That is life. May God be thanked!"

They lay down. Amor pressed himself against Aïcha. He felt good after a day at the beach.

"Our oldest son is a man like his father!"

He laughed and took his wife in his arms. A few images of women he had seen on the beach passed through his mind, legs, and breasts, how magnificent! But it was with the familiar body of Aïcha, his wife, that he liked to make love. Any other body would intimidate him, perhaps paralyze him; Aïcha's body fulfilled him; his desire bloomed next to it, and was satisfied by it. May God be praised! May Hocine find his wife's body, man's greatest happiness.

'My daughter, aren't you feeling a bit tired lately?''
Fatiha looked up at her mother-in-law.
"I'm not tired. I feel just fine."
Fatiha continued peeling the potatoes; they were both
in the courtyard under the fig tree with a large pan between
them in which they threw the peeled and cut pieces. The
habitual gestures that Aïcha repeated day in and day out
without weariness.
"You... You aren't late with your period?"
Fatiha carried on as if she had not heard. Aïcha took her
by the hand.
"Fatiha, tell me..."
Fatiha pulled her hand away and responded brusquely
"That's... that's my business!"
Aïcha was astounded. She dropped her knife in the pan
and yelled: "Fatiha, you have no respect for me!"
With that she began crying, sincerely hurt by this
answer. Hocine had come in just in time to hear his
mother's last sentence. He saw his wife and his mother
eyeing each other; without asking a single question he
grabbed Fatiha's arm violently, as if he were grabbing a
child, and took her towards their bedroom shaking her as
they went.
"You must not show disrespect for my mother! I will
never tolerate that, do you hear me!"
Aïcha continued to wail in the courtyard. Ali and
Néfissa, who were playing in the house, stuck their heads
out the door. Fatiha did not allow herself to be dragged
easily.
"You don't even know what happened!"
Hocine, overcome by Fatiha's resistance, slapped her.
Fatiha looked at him with anger, abruptly broke away and
ran off; she slammed the door of their room in Hocine's
face. Allaoua and Yamina came in, attracted by their
mother's lamenting, and saw the scene. Amor, who had
also just come in, asked what was happening. Allaoua

stepped towards Hocine. Hocine pushed him back and left rapidly. Aïcha wanted to stop her eldest son from leaving.

"Where are you going, my son?"

He left without answering her; she stood a moment looking at the gateway, then came back into the house; Fatiha locked herself in the room. Allaoua kicked the ball the children had in the middle of the courtyard violently. Yamina timidly knocked at Fatiha's door, trying not to be noticed. She went in. Fatiha was sitting on the mattress crying. Yamina walked towards her and gave her an affectionate kiss on the top of her head.

"It's nothing, my friend, my sister."

Fatiha looked up at Yamina.

"He hit me and without a reason! I'll never accept being beaten! Never!"

Yamina continued to stroke her hair and then put her face against Fatiha's.

"Don't cry, my sister. . . don't cry. . . aren't you happy with Hocine? Why? He's not mean! He's nervous but he's not mean; I'm sure he's not mean."

"We don't understand each other, Yamina! We don't really know each other; we don't talk to each other. . . I didn't want to get married like that!"

"I'd like you to be happy so much!"

"We aren't happy and I don't think we can be. . ."

"Don't talk like that!"

Fatiha smiled at her young sister-in-law who seemed so helpless and in turn caressed her face and hair. I would like to go back to my parents', she thought, but she did not say it.

Hocine was walking nervously in the street. He was so irritated by the scene and the slap he had given his wife that he could have given her a second one, just like that, without any explanation, if she were there at his side.

Irritated with his parents who had obliged him to

marry. Angry with life, the way it was when you wanted it to be completely different. Angry with Fatiha who was not the woman he should have married. Angry with himself. He headed towards the fish market. It was not the first time he had gone there to see if there was any work for him.

"Ah, yes, Hocine! Good morning. I'm sorry. I'm sorry. I would have like to have pleased your father so much! But really, at this time it's impossible; next month, maybe. . ."

"I'll come back, thank you."

The director of the market cordially shook Hocine's hand and smiled, then left rapidly like a man in a hurry. Hocine left slowly. He crossed the whole length of the market. He looked at the stalls full of fresh fish; a man offered him some; he hesitated; if he bought any he would have to go straight back to the house but he felt like walking near the sea. He stopped again before a fish that was still alive and fighting suffocation, shining, full of light and yet so close to death. Hocine lit a cigarette and left. Anyway, he would not like working there very much. . .fish that never stopped dying, the smell of fish all day long!. . .He was amused by his reaction. . .as if Paris smelled good, in the metro! Long live the fish market! Long live the sun! Long live the sea!

A few meters away was a man in his forties, busy picking up the garbage and papers thrown on the sand. He had just piled up empty soda and beer bottles a little further on. He stabbed a paper with his pointed metal cane and came towards Hocine with a jovial air. He felt like having a little chat and Hocine seemed friendly.

"You went to the fish market for work?"

Hocine, surprised, nodded yes.

"I saw you there! There's no work! He told you to come back? He says that to everybody. . .He says that all the time! But no use in coming back 'cause when there's work it's for Si Djebar's friends. That's the way it is! I work here. City Hall pays me. I clean the beach; in the afternoon

I sell beans and olives. . .That's the way it is! Work, if you look in the right places you'll find some, but you have to be ready to do anything! I've been a shepherd, I've shined shoes, I've been a gardener, I know how to do everything, I even know how to repair electricity!"

Hocine looked at him kindly. This man needed to talk to someone he didn't know, so Hocine listened. From time to time he desired to talk to a stranger too, to say everything on his mind, but he had lost the habit of speaking and confiding. . .

"Oh, yeah. . .That's the way it is. Misery taught me everything in life, everything!"

With that the man began diligently picking up papers.

"It's different for me, but I'm working for my children. I still got four going to school. I don't want them to be like me, maybe one day one of them will strike it rich!"

He laughed and then his face grew dim.

"Last month, believe it or not, I didn't even make enough to send to my wife; I make so little! She stayed back in the village. Are you married?"

"Yes."

"Got any children?"

"No, not yet."

"You will, if God wishes!"

The man walked off cleaning the ground and talking to himself.

"I haven't heard from her at all; maybe she asked for a divorce like her mother wanted her to! The cursed woman!"

Hocine watched the man walk off, then turn suddenly and give a big friendly wave of the hand.

"May God help you!"

Hocine smiled and brought his hand to his heart; the man continued to work, happy to have talked to someone; Hocine left slowly.

Sometimes when he was home from abroad Hocine

would reacquire that slow walk he had before, when he used to imitate his father; a slow walk that calmed the body and the mind; even those thoughts that obsess would slow their rhythm and sometimes disappear.

Hocine followed the shoreline for a few hundred meters from the market and then sat at a café terrace, ordered a beer and lit a cigarette; he watched the people pass; a young couple with a baby who was entranced by a multicolored propeller he was playing with. The young mother was not much older than Fatiha; she was holding her husband's arm; she was not wearing a veil. His memories of France overshadowed, or rather formed the backdrop, mixing with the images of the present. He contemplated everything around him while going with the rhythm of the memories of his life in Paris. Here and there at the same time. Suddenly he was walking with a friend in the densely populated streets of Place Clichy:

"You see, I can't do without Paris and this neighborhood any more; I'm not happy here but I'm not happy back home either; try to make some sense out of that! Completely addicted to it, like tobacco. . . over two packs a day, my man! They say it gives you cancer. . . you have to die from something. . . those that don't smoke die too!"

Hocine remained silent as usual.

"What do you like in life?" his friend asked and Hocine answered:

"Oh. . . if only I knew! One day it's one thing or another and the next it's something else or nothing at all. . ."

"You, my brother, must have wanted something pretty badly at one time and you were let down! That can happen to you afterwards!"

Hocine had never forgotten this conversation; it came back to him like that, unexpectedly, and it always provoked a number of related ideas and images. Today it was associated with one of his friends hurt at the construction site. Why? Ah. . . because he knew what he wanted! But life had decided otherwise. Hocine thought of Fatiha, of the slap, of her angry look. He wondered what it was she could have said to his mother. . . Ah. . . women! He would ask her that night. He saw a veiled woman walking heavily and leading two children by the hand while another trotted by provocatively in high-heeled shoes. He recalled Marie-Laure whom he had seen for two years in Paris. He met her when she was a saleswoman at Uniprix; she had just left her family; he could remember her smiling face and her angry one as well. Their relationship had been a stormy one, with sun, black clouds and thunder. . .

"If you don't trust me then get out of here! Get out of here!"

If he had not been so jealous she would not have left him. But it was stronger than he was.

"That's all you all are really capable of, possessing a woman like you would a dog! Your property! Why not on a leash while you're at it?"

Hocine thought it was more a question of respect than one of property, yes, respect! To be respected! He had told her that, and she had answered the obvious:

"You're not the only one who wants to be respected; I want to be respected too!"

He knew she was right. We all need to be respected, he thought. But then how does one go about it? They said things to each other that provoked the separation, a separation neither one of them wanted. . . Hocine ordered another beer and lit another cigarette.

Fatiha was sitting on the bed in the semi-darkness. She could hear the noise in the next room but paid no attention. Her heart and her body were too full of painful questions, questions without answers; the present was like an impenetrable wall which she kept banging against, so she began to daydream. She remembered the evening she had chatted with her sister rather than going to sleep.

"Fatiha...Fatiha, tonight the spirits are listening!"

"What spirits?"

"The spirits of the night, the ones that bring happiness your whole life because it's the first day of summer. Let's count and the last one will be the one who gets the best husband..."

They counted and laughed.

Their mother and grandmother came in:

"Oh, they're sleeping like angels, the dear little things!"

They tiptoed away. As soon as the door had closed the game began again. Fatiha was the last. She would get the best husband! Hocine...the best husband! How long ago these childish fantasies were and yet still so close in her heart. Fatiha could see the affectionate face of her mother and the laughing faces of her two sisters and young brother. Why all that tenderness if it was only to be abruptly taken away? She had a great desire to see her parents again; she knew if they did not come to see her it was not because they lived on the other side of the city but because she had to get used to her new family and her new home. But she was not getting used to it, and she had the feeling she never would. She imagined herself in a house that was completely hers and her husband's, and Hocine a little different from what he was. He smiled at her. They talked to each other. He was interested in her seamstress work. She had a lot of work; the women in the neighborhood came to her home; their children ran around the house; she walked freely in the street without a veil; she went shopping; she went into the bookstore and chose a book and a fashion catalog. She and Hocine kissed, chatted and laughed.

Allaoua sat in the courtyard waiting for Hocine with some trepidation. He had decided to speak to him about Fatiha and about what had happened. He had been gathering strength ever since he had made his decision; he thought about what he would say to him...he was worried. His eldest brother was not easy to approach and he knew how daring his decision was. It was already dark. Hocine came in. Allaoua went quickly to meet him.

"What are you doing there?"

"I was waiting for you."

"Waiting for me? Why? What's the matter?"

"I wanted...I wanted...to speak to you about Fatiha, about what happened this afternoon between you and her..."

Hocine, at first worried, then suddenly furious over his younger brother's audacity, pushed him away and went on.

"What right do you have? Mind your own business! Go to bed!"

Hocine controlled his exasperation with great difficulty; he almost slapped him. Allaoua remained in the center of the courtyard motionless, fixed, distressed. His older brother was decidedly not easy to deal with. He would have liked to be a friend and be able to talk to him about everything. But that was impossible. Why should it be impossible?

Hocine abruptly entered his room. He was furious over what had just happened with Allaoua. Fatiha quickly sat up while Hocine turned on the lights.

"What are you doing in the dark like that?"

"I was waiting for you."

Hocine hung his jacket up and without looking at her:

"Why were you disrespectful to my mother?"

"I wasn't disrespectful to her."

Fatiha's voice was calm, almost indifferent.

"Are you saying my mother lied?"

"I got upset when she asked me something I couldn't tell her."

"What did she ask you that you couldn't tell her?"

Hocine, surprised, was now facing her. She was not looking at him; she was seated with her hands crossed on her knees; her long hair fell freely over her blue dress. She remained silent.

"What couldn't you tell her, Fatiha?"

"She asked me if I was getting my periods. . ."

Hocine, astonished, approached and lifted up her head forcing her to look at him.

"You don't get them?"

Fatiha again lowered her head breaking away from Hocine's hand.

"Fatiha, tomorrow you will tell my mother you are pregnant. . . and you will apologize."

He spoke to her softly. Fatiha looked at him astonished; his tone was emotional; but that was all he found to say: you will apologize. . . For a moment she became dizzy; her head was spinning; then she stiffened and undressed without a word.

Hocine was deeply moved by the news but he let nothing show. His wife was pregnant. He would be a father. He had not accepted the marriage, he had not accepted the duty of paternity. The women he had known had all had abortions. He wanted this child with all his soul, yet unconsciously rejected it with as much strength as he desired it. He smoked cigarette after cigarette unable to go to sleep, unable to reach out to his wife.

Fatiha remained awake and still at his side.

You'll tell her you're pregnant and you'll apologize. . . You'll tell her. . . You'll apologize. . . I'm going to have a baby. . . I'm going to have a baby and Hocine is his father. . .

Why couldn't he understand that she had to get used to the idea herself first?

Why didn't he understand that they should have been able to tell each other?

We're going to have a baby. . .

Man's sex. Man's raving. Man's pleasure.

I'm going to have a baby.

This as yet unhealed wound of body and soul.

Fatiha let out a cry and felt like vomiting.

Under the affectionate pressure of his parents Hocine tried in every possible and imaginable way to find work before finally deciding to return to France. He crisscrossed Algiers from one end to the other, a city he had become very fond of and felt so good in. Algiers, its sun, its crowds, its women in cloaks surrounded by swarms of children, its animation, its life, so much more human than Paris was, so much warmer, so much gayer; and also the impression of being at home, not noticed, not noticeable, not rejected, not excluded. This was where his wife and children must live, nowhere else. Because he felt this attachment to Algiers more strongly than in the first days of his return he looked for work with ever greater determination; but he could find none.

One day, tired of the endless attempts to find work, he went for a walk in the Casbah. Children who were jumping four steps at a time in a street of stairs gathered around him laughing. An old man sitting on a doorstoop watched.

"Hey you, my brother, you're a tourist in your own country! Are you looking for something? Maybe I can help you."

"No thank you, I'm not looking for anything."

"You're always looking for something, my brother!"

Hocine smiled at the old man and walked on. The old man, wrapped in an old and worn out djellaba, nodded his head.

"A tourist in his own country!" Hocine turned around. The old man was no longer watching him. "You're always looking for something, my brother!" Yes. . . he was looking for something. . . first of all for work which he could not find. Work, here, in this city. And he was looking. . . for what else? "You're always looking for something, my brother!. . ."

A bit further two young kids were squaring off and threatening to break each other's heads. Some others were trying to dissuade them. They fight in the streets of France too. They fight everywhere. Is it because men like to fight? Or is it because they are looking for something they haven't found?

Hocine covered the city and saw it as it was, swarming, alive, poor and rich at the same time. Overcrowded buildings, all too often badly kept; too many broken windows, too many cracked walls with too much graffiti here and there and even some old inscriptions from the War of Liberation, some from the O.A.S., badly hidden by strokes of paint too quickly applied. The city, full of construction sites where there is no hiring; the city full of space for future buildings; full of those who work and those who don't, trying to survive by hustling. Something found here and sold there. Look! Well, look! That's giving it away! A watch like this. . . you can swim with it, knock it about. . . you do anything with it! Transistor radios. . .

No, he would not become a little hustler. And those children begging! There should not be any children, nor elderly, forced to beg in our country. . . It shouldn't be any more. . . It shouldn't be any more. . . Between what should not be and what was! There are beggars everywhere. . . "You mustn't give them anything, it encourages the vice!" He had given money to a gypsy child one day in the Paris subway and he was struck by the looks from those around him.

Hocine went to all the addresses different people had given him. Everywhere they asked him to fill out papers and still more papers; he didn't know how to write. He could have brought his wife along with him; she knew how to write, she knew; but he refused to and therefore needed the good will of someone every time. "We'll let you know...but don't expect anything soon." Always the same answer..."Don't expect anything..."

He tried his luck at the port. Nothing. Always nothing. But how magnificent the port was! One could stay for hours looking at it. He sat at the terrace of a café. Whether he sat down or went on looking for work...the result was the same. He looked at the succession of docks where the blue played with the sky and the bright colors of the ships; then further out, the sea. A score of boats waited to be unloaded. They say the country loses a million a day! What a waste if it's true!

At one of the corners of the square dozens of men and women were waiting for taxis which never seemed to stop. Hocine was amused by those who called, yelled, pushed and shoved; those who ran out in front of every yellow car that looked like a taxi trying to butt ahead of everybody. They butt in line everywhere; the buses were taken by assault and left jampacked. It was really worse than Paris! Some old men dozing in the shade, hidden under the hoods of their burnouse, indifferent to all the agitation. Women passed nonchalantly or in a hurry. Children were running, shouting and having fun. At the café, on the terrace and inside, there were only men; but Hocine paid no attention to the exclusion of women. However he did notice a veiled woman of about forty, standing on the sidewalk, drinking a coffee that a little boy, her son or her grandson, had gone in to get her. The child was waiting to take the empty cup back to the counter. A European woman, ignoring their customs, entered and sat at a table among all the men; she ordered a coffee, lit a cigarette, and admired the port.

Hocine felt good on the terrace; the bright light reflected by the stone and water quieted his thoughts; he forgot his worries. Hocine was not daydreaming; he had not daydreamed since his friend, Boudjema, died at Nanterre. Boudjema had dreamt nonstop. He saw himself coming back home with enough money to buy a small business, a house, get married and have children. If working could not guarantee him all that, off track betting would make up the difference. Boudjema was so confident. But life had decided differently! Or rather. . . death had. . . Hocine thought often about death since then. At this moment Hocine was thinking of nothing, not of death, nor of life, nor of the child to be born, nor of Fatiha, nor that he was unemployed here in his own country; nor that he was an immigrant worker in France; nor did he think about how he was always reduced to this one social status while he was really something completely different; a complex man, like all men, he could not be reduced to work, to the absence of work, to filling out papers, to things asked of him that he was ignorant of, while what he did know was never asked. At this moment he was smoking, looking about, forgetting everything that had to be forgotten in order to live a few privileged moments; moments where one feels closer to things, more alive as well as more human.

"I looked, father! Really, for two months that's all I've done! I've been everywhere I could go."

"Look some more, my son. You'll find something eventually. There's no hurry."

Hocine and his father were having coffee in the large sitting room. Some light modern music came from the radio. They were sitting on the only two armchairs, which were draped in handmade covers to hide the worn out fabric.

"Look some more, my son. Look some more!"

"I told you I would come back home for three months

and get married, according to your wishes and that I would go back to France where I have work."

"Are you really sure you'll get this job back?"

"That was the agreement."

"But your place is here, my son, with your wife; here, with us, especially now that you are going to be a father. I am so happy to have you here. You'll find work. Everything is changing in our country, you've seen that. I can help you in the meantime, you know that. We aren't rich but it is better to sacrifice a little and live together, isn't it? You know we have always shared here!"

His father's voice was warm and Hocine smiled at him.

"Father, if I'd found work I would've stayed, but I haven't found any. I must go back to France; my boss promised me I would get my job again when I got there; I don't have anything here; when there's work here I'll come back. Meanwhile I'll send you money like before; it's better that way. Fatiha will stay with you and the child will be born here."

It was as if he were offering the child to his parents.

Amor remained silent for a long moment, deep in thought, annoyed, then making an effort:

"My son, I didn't tell you but I've been making a lot of applications for you without success. I fought for our country, as you know; there are those who did nothing, who were hiding abroad and now they have good jobs! Why? Try to make sense out of that! Do you see, my son, it's not right, no, it's not right. None of those men with good jobs would give me one for you; even though I had never asked for anything before! Never!"

Aïcha had entered a few seconds before and heard her husband's last few words. Judging from the expression on their faces she guessed that Hocine had decided to leave for France again. She took a cloth from the large cupboard and left, slamming the door.

"It's not going to be easy talking to your mother! She wanted you to stay with us so much!"

"I think she has already guessed!"

Hocine was relieved that they'd finally gotten things out on the table. It had to be done. He contemplated the smoke from his cigarette; his father observed him with affection.

"Are you happy, my son?"

"Of course, father . . ."

"Good, I'm relieved. May God be blessed! Our tradition has merit in spite of what the young say. I know well that we all have different desires within us, and that's just it, we've got too many. When they married me off I loved one of my cousins; but my parents didn't want that marriage because they had this squabble with her parents . . . a family squabble! That didn't stop me from being happy with your mother. A marriage is like planting a tree; you have to know how to protect it! Your brother says he wants to choose for himself, but you don't choose your country, you don't choose your mother, they are given to you; you don't choose your century, it's given to you. Everything is decided elsewhere, my son! And if we don't like what life has offered us then we risk losing ourselves, we risk passing life by, we risk passing God by. Isn't that right, my son?"

Hocine was moved as he was every time his father spoke to him with that intensity he had, that truth, that calm assurance that he would have liked so much to share with him. Hocine looked at his father in silence.

The two men remained silent a long moment.

While Amor and Hocine were talking, smoking, and drinking coffee, Fatiha was preparing biscuits for the evening. Squatting in the kitchen near the gas burner, the sleeves of her kabyle dress rolled up to the elbows and her hair tucked under a blue scarf, she rolled, mixed, and tapped the dough from one hand to the other with lively and precise movements, then flattened a doughball in the palm of her hand and quickly spread it on the hotplate, turning it over and over, completely immersed in her work. The golden biscuits were piled on top of each other on a cloth at her feet. She did not hear Aïcha coming, nervously rumpling the cloth she had just taken from the cupboard. She jumped with a start at her mother-in-law's loud violent voice.

"Hocine is going back to France! It's all your fault! You didn't know how to hold my son here!"

Fatiha turned in surprise and met the anger-filled eyes of Aïcha. She looked away and went back to making biscuits.

"You make my son miserable!"

Fatiha's attitude of apparent indifference irritated Aïcha more than anything.

"Did you hear me?"

Fatiha, pushed to the limit, threw the dough on the biscuits violently; she got up, dried her hands, walked by Aïcha, and left the kitchen. Aïcha was taken aback and remained in the middle of the room.

"She's going to lock herself in her room again! That's all she knows how to do! Ah, a curse is on this house!"

Aïcha let herself fall into a chair where she sat feeling sorry for herself; then she quickly stood up and went in to the courtyard still holding onto the piece of cloth she intended to mend. Little Ali, with his curly hair, pink face, and constant laugh, ran up to his mother, threw himself at her dress and hid his head as he always did. Néfissa was bouncing a ball off the wall. Yamina was sitting under the fig tree unstitching the lapels of one of Allaoua's vests; she remained silent as she did every time they were on the brink of a tragedy or already plunging into one. It seemed to her that silence could avoid making things worse, although at times, it did just the opposite. Since her eldest brother's marriage to Fatiha, Yamina had borne the multiplying ten-

sions, conflicts, and misunderstandings with great difficulty. Very young, sensitive, idealist and passive, she would
have liked the days to pass without confrontation, without
anger. Aïcha, seeing that her daughter was not going to ask
what had happened, left rapidly for her son's room. She
broke in. Fatiha yielded her the place and went out without
a word, without a glance.

"You play the proud one because you went to school!
What good is it if you can't keep your husband?"

Fatiha went back to the kitchen looking like she was
not paying attention, when in reality she could barely control her anger. Hocine, having heard the outbursts, arrived
and found himself face to face with his mother.

"What's the matter?"

"Your wife is disrespectful to me! She runs around so
proud and you let her do it; she could care less about
anything I say!"

"You're the one who wanted my marriage, not me!"

He spoke as loudly as his mother did and Fatiha heard
everything.

"May God be witness that I only wanted what was
good for you!"

Hocine left.

Aïcha intensified her laments. Overwhelmed by the
conflicts and the mood of the moment, she was profoundly
unhappy and sure she had good reason to be. She felt as if
her eldest son had just been torn away from her and she was
suffering to the depths of her soul. So somebody had to be
responsible!

Amor, who had just left, heard nothing.

As for Allaoua, before leaving he yelled loudly and de-
fiantly:

"That's what you get with tradition!"

Yamina, deep in thought, was wondering what exactly
had happened. . . who was right, who was wrong? She had

the feeling something had just broken that they would not be able to put back together. She would have liked to go to her young sister-in-law, whom she loved dearly, but she dared not for fear of embittering the situation and irritating her mother. She remained seated, her work on her lap, on the brink of tears, confused and full of repressed impulses. The children began playing with a ball and, to be in harmony with everyone else, were now yelling and arguing.

Hocine had jumped in the first bus that came along and was now in the center of Algiers; automatically, he stopped in front of a newspaper stand, looked at a few news photos without the least bit of interest and began walking towards Didouch Mourad street. Having made and announced his decision to go back to France, he felt a certain freedom. This completely fruitless job-seeking had become a burden and was extremely irritating. The indecision was also aggravating; and then he had to admit it to himself, family life was difficult after having spent so many years away. At first it had been the irresistible chain of festivities and, in spite of all the contradictions involved in his so little wished-for marriage, he had felt as if he were on vacation. He savored all the happiness, all the warmth of family get-togethers. But, having adopted so many foreign ways, the multiple constraints of home life very quickly pressed in on him.

In Didouch Mourad street, full of people as usual, Hocine met his friends Salah and Mohamed; they embraced each other with joy, had a coffee together, thought about going to the movies and then changed their minds. They would go to the beach instead. Hocine accepted Salah's suggestion with delight; soon he would no longer be able to go to the beach. Vacation would be over!

Ah, if only we could take a bus thirty kilometers from Paris and find the sea, a beach of fine sand, the sun! With a laugh he said to Salah:

"My friend, take advantage of the sea while you are here! When you get to Paris you will have to do without!"

Fatiha locked herself in her room and began writing a letter to her friend Myriem whom she had not seen since the wedding.

"Myriem, come and see me; I beg you, come. . . I need so much to speak to you! Come. . . come. . . My husband is going back to France; he's going to leave me alone, here, with his parents. His mother blames me for his departure, but it has nothing to do with me. He beat me because of his mother, and for that I will never forgive him. Come, Myriem, I need so much to see you. I'm expecting a baby. . ."

She wrote the letter just as the ideas came to her head and then stopped; she felt the urge to tear it up and only ask Myriem to come see her. But she did not have the courage. She did not have the courage to tear this letter up, nor the courage to write another note, nor the courage to write her parents, something she had sworn to do. She would send this letter just the way it was! But how could she send it? The only way was to give it to Allaoua.

Hocine and his friends spent a few hours at the beach, absorbed in the pleasures of swimming, tanning under the sun, breathing the fresh sea air, and admiring the changing colors. They ate melon and figs and shared a chicken. A true holiday.

A very beautiful Ford stopped not far from them. The three friends looked at it. Two couples got out and headed for the sea, holding hands with their arms around each other's waists. Salah only saw the women and gave a sigh of admiration. The men and women ran into the sea together, swam, enjoyed themselves, laughed, kissed. Hocine stood up abruptly, as if annoyed by the newcomers, and dressed. Salah and Mohamed, following his example, shook the sand off their backs and legs and got dressed. They passed the Ford on the way off the beach and Mohamed stopped and walked around the car admiring it.

"How much does a toy like this cost?"

"You never lack women with a car like that!"

Salah had no training, no work, no wife, no girlfriend, and resorting to prostitutes— who were plentiful in Algiers, as elsewhere—humiliated him...so...the car really interested him less than the women did! He would prefer the most modest woman to the most extraordinary car!

Hocine was neither interested in this deluxe car nor in these inaccesible women of a different milieu. One of the swimmers was for a moment worried by the presence of the three men around the car, but seeing them leave, turned again to his beautiful companion.

The three friends walked down streets lined with magnificent villas, set deep within their sumptuous gardens.

"Maybe there's a cheap place for rent in this neighborhood," Mohamed said with a laugh.

"Sure, we can ask if you'd like!"

Salah laughed. What would I do with such a villa and no wife? Of course, it's true that if I had a villa like that I would also have a wife!

The Ford they had looked at back on the beach passed by slowly with its four joyful occupants. It stopped in front of one of the very good restaurants in this fancy resort area. Other cars arrived. It was the time of dinner rendezvous, of friendly meals in a Thousand And One Nights' setting. The three friends stopped in front of one of the posted menus searching for the prices, then glanced inside, soft-colored lights reflecting off the stuccoes. Some people were already being seated for dinner, some tourists as well, national and international privileged people.

"Doesn't it make you hungry? Come on, I'll buy you a sausage at the first shish kabob seller, if there is one!"

Hocine and Salah laughed.

"Let's go!"

It was late when Hocine got home after a long day with his friends. Fatiha was combing her hair in front of the mirror; she turned towards him; he had that relaxed face of a man who had spent the day at the beach with his friends and appeared to have forgotten everything that had happened in the beginning of the afternoon. He turned on the radio. They were broadcasting the last minutes of a soccer match. He sat down, listened for a moment, then lay back.

"So, you're going back to France soon?"

She asked the question calmly but firmly.

"I haven't found any work here; I always said I would go back if I couldn't find work here."

"Are you taking me with you?"

"No, Fatiha, no!"

"You're going to leave me here, alone, pregnant?"

"I'm not leaving you alone. I'm leaving you with my parents. A lot of people would love to be part of such a family. Here you're considered as one of the children of the house; you can be happy if you want to. You have to get along with my mother. She doesn't have your outlook on life, but she's a good woman and her anger is quickly forgotten. And on top of that she would be an excellent example for you to follow, in every way."

He spoke quickly, brusquely, and Fatiha guessed his irritation. She lay back on the bed and then propped herself up.

"Hocine, I beg you, don't leave me here alone. Take me! I beg you!" She spoke gravely.

Hocine, surprised, even more irritated by her grave tone of voice which he didn't understand, answered nervously:

"You cannot come with me, Fatiha, I have already told you and I'm telling you again. France is no country for you.

It's already hard enough for a man to live there, for a woman it's even worse! You have no idea! You would be lonelier there than you are here! I would leave you very early in the morning and I'd get back very late at night. What would you do by yourself all day?"

"There are those who take their wives and their children with them. There are those who go and can't even speak French; I speak it, I read it, I write it. . . ."

Hocine looked at Fatiha intensely. She appealed to him this evening; he desired her and was irritated by her stubborn resistance.

"No, Fatiha! No, no, no! You are well off here and you'll never go without."

Fatiha turned away and fell silent. He put his hand on her breast. She broke away violently and sat on the edge of the bed turning her back to him.

"My mother was right, Fatiha, you have a lousy temperament! And the less I remain here, the better it will be for us all."

He got dressed and left the room. Fatiha did not say a word. At that moment she despised him. She despised this force and it's not taking her desires into consideration at all, this will that decided for her and against her. Let him go! She wouldn't care! But as soon as the thought had crossed her mind, she again realized with certainty that the only way out of this life they wanted to impose on her here was to leave for France with her husband. In Paris they would live alone together. Perhaps he'd change if they lived somewhere else and could be free, just the two of them, and later, with the child? Perhaps they could even learn to love each other? Perhaps she could work? She wished for this agreement with all her heart, after all they were husband and wife and she felt so awful in this vacuum of affection, in this situation, so unforeseen, so incomprehensible. She would have preferred so much more to be able to build a real home with him, suitable for receiving their child.

Hocine walked in the courtyard smoking a cigarette and, from time to time, he looked at the sky; it was nice out. He recalled his arrival a few weeks earlier; so recent and yet so long ago. The taxi had slowed and stopped in front of their house. It hadn't changed a bit. It would never change. That was one thing he was sure of, and he found it reassuring. His mother was waiting with tear-filled eyes, all tenderness, all love. Her indescribable, unforgettable look, that marvelous look of maternal love. His father, dignified as always, moved and happy, so happy that his eldest son was back, so happy that he had finally agreed to marry; his father, unchanged as well, defender of the traditions he believed in, as much as he believed in God. His little brother, Ali, laughing to the point of tears, everyone so happy to see each other again. And the timid, pretty Néfissa, and Yamina. . . Yamina, what a surprise!. . . He had left her a child and now she was a young lady, a discreet young lady full of charm. He had taken out the gifts one by one while the little ones ran all around clapping their hands. Allaoua examined his new camera from every angle, almost undone with excitement.

He had also left him when he was only a child and now he was almost a man with his own ideas about everything. . . Yamina, unfolding the material, his mother crying for joy, wearing her new wrist watch. ''We have missed you, my son. All these gifts, you shouldn't have, my son!'' He remembered that day when he sat next to his mother under the fig tree with the large leaves. It was very hot; Fatiha served them coffee; his mother hugged him like she did when he was a child. At that moment Hocine was overcome with the desire for tenderness, the desire to make love; he threw down his cigarette and went back to their bedroom. Fatiha was in bed; he got in bed, put his arms around her.

Fatiha was ignorant about everything concerning sex; she was surprised with herself for permitting a man's pleasure when she experienced none. She discovered man's enjoyment, that solitary enjoyment, that fullness which forgot her but that could not exist without her. She had not discovered her own enjoyment—did she have any?—but rather a bit more about a woman's powers, a bit more of her loneliness. It seemed to her that she knew Hocine better. But her own body remained mysterious, full of resistance, full of desire, full of expectation, incomprehensible, elusive, this body that was now secretly making a child. Her body and heart, so demanding and yet so unsatisfied.

"What are you doing here?"
"We've just come from the stadium."
"And your job training school?"
"Today is Thursday."
"Thursday? Oh, yes, that's right."
Hocine and Allaoua had just bumped into each other by chance. Allaoua waved to his friends and began walking with his brother.
"When you finish your job training do you think you'll find some work?"
"That's what the training is for; the factory will hire me next year."
"That's good."
"So, you're leaving again?"
"Yes."
Allaoua hesitated to speak to Hocine about his coming departure; there was so little possibility of talking to him, he seemed so closed off. There was so little friendly camaraderie between them; Hocine always seemed to be on his guard and so quick to become hostile.
"You didn't find any work?"

"No, you know that!"

"You're leaving?...your wife is going to have a baby..."

He was being awkward and realized it immediately. Hocine started.

"You're still worrying about my wife, even now? Mind your own business!"

"Ah, don't get angry; we can talk, can't we..."

"About something else, yes, if you want! Mind your own business! What do you know about life? When I was your age I shut up."

"That's just it...things have changed!"

"That's just it, they haven't!"

Hocine stopped and looked his young brother straight in the eyes, extremely irritated. They sized each other up, opposed each other, incapable of dialogue. Hocine abruptly left Allaoua and walked off without looking back. Allaoua remained still and watched his brother walk away, then quickly turned back towards his friends who were still talking in the same place. Allaoua, agitated and angered, joined his friends.

"What's the matter? Is something wrong?" Allaoua's best friend, Mokhtar, asked.

"It...it's...my brother's going back to France! He looked for work and didn't find any. They married him to a girl my age; they had never seen each other before the wedding and don't seem to enjoy seeing each other now! A marriage like in the old days! It's as if nothing has changed in the past fifty years in my family!"

"I know all that, but what else?"

"What else? He's going back; his wife is pregnant; she's not happy with us...I would never accept that...never!"

"Neither would I," Mokhtar said.

"Oh," Saïd joined in, "I knew some who said that and then...they gave in; because you have to admit that women who don't follow tradition are not easy...You don't know how to handle them..."

"When you let women be free, they abuse it. Tradition or not," Khaleb said, "I won't marry a woman who's not a virgin! Even if I love her!"

"Yeah, sure, but when you find a woman to make love to you're happy! That's just hypocritical, that's all! And what purpose do all those prejudices serve?"

Allaoua had answered Khaleb with force. That his brother, from a completely different generation, acted the way he did was barely comprehensible, but that his friends could still be in the same place made him furious; he felt like leaving them there and going off by himself. Tahar, guessing his mood and not having much of an idea himself about what he would or would not do when it came to marriage...which was not an immediate question...hurried to change the conversation.

"You're always talking about women! Change the record! Speaking of records, let's go to Abel's, he's got a far-out hi-fi and lots of records...Wait till you see, it's far out..."

"O.K., let's go!"

They began to walk rapidly in the direction of the miracle records that had the power to make one forget everything else. They passed the old man who had rigged up a camera with tin cans. He looked like he was straight out of one of those yellowed, antique photographs, with that big black cloth over his head and the camera, like in the old days. Allaoua and his friends paused, then went on.

"You know, when you see that and you look at the tourist's cameras!" Mokhtar said.

"And what about those they're selling at Hamou's in Emir Abdelkader Square...Have you seen them? It'll be a while before I can get myself a Rolley automatic. Photography is my passion, not women!"

"You can't get everything at once!"

"One doesn't exclude the other."

"While you're waiting to buy one, make yourself one with tin cans!"

Allaoua and his friends laughed. He found the camera that his brother had brought him from France very beautiful but he had not used it very much because film was so expensive. He did not mention it because he did not want to lend it out, because what you lend you are never sure of getting back...

He was a bit ashamed to think like that... He would lend it to Mokhtar... nobody else... He liked photography too. They would learn to take beautiful pictures and then learn how to enlarge them—you need more equipment for that—and then they would show their pictures... at that moment he thought he would like to photograph women's faces, a lot of women's faces.

A quarter of an hour later the whole band was at Abdel's, crowded into the small room he shared with his two brothers. Disco music with the volume all the way up. Dancing in place, among boys, in four square meters of free space! The slightly crazy rhythm absorbed everything: desires, suppressed feelings, worries, disappointments. Abdel's mother stuck her head in the door.

"Couldn't you make a bit less noise?"

The boys broke out laughing but paid no attention to the remark. Healthy excitement! Rhythms and sounds until the body collapsed and the mind blanked out.

Fatiha was preparing Hocine's things. She put in a few more items and slid a picture of their wedding between two shirts. Hocine came in the room and sat on the bed as if he was very tired.

"Is it ready?"

"Yes."

He waved her to come and sit beside him. She obeyed. They remained side by side in silence for a long moment; then Hocine put his hand on Fatiha's and looked at her tenderly.

"Fatiha, I've got to leave in order to work. You won't be unhappy here. I've spoken with my mother, she's only interested in your well-being." Fatiha looked at him in silence.

"Things in France aren't like you all imagine them here. You think life there is easy but you're dreaming! I can't take you with me because I live with four friends in one small room. Rents are very high in Paris; we couldn't get a decent place with the money I make. I can't take you with me because they don't like us there, they don't respect us, and I could never tolerate that you weren't respected!"

She listened in silence, moved. He had never spoken to her like he was doing this evening; she did not feel that she had been respected the way she would have wished; yet he wanted her to be respected! Then everything was possible. This seemed to open all the doors at once. Maybe one day they would be able to get along, listen to each other, understand each other? She undressed and slid into bed.

"Let's go to bed, you have to rest for the trip; you're leaving very early tomorrow."

Hocine had never heard Fatiha speak to him in this way; it seemed to him that she was a woman, for the first time he had the impression that she accepted him as he was and he was grateful to her. But tonight he was incapable of taking her into his arms. He lay back in bed completely dressed, smoking cigarette after cigarette. Why was his life like this with departures and uprootings? Were they imposed on him? Did he provoke them? He no longer knew. He did not know if he wanted to stay with Fatiha or if he preferred to leave her. He was happy to be leaving, yet somewhere within him there was pain and he really didn't know what it was that was hurting him. At that instant his life seemed to consist of moments not linked to each other, completely dissimilar, with no continuity.

Early the following morning Hocine left, accompanied by his younger brother who carried the biggest suitcase. Aïcha was crying with one hand over her mouth as if to stop the sounds. The little ones, already up, held her dress tight against her. Amor, silent, sad, a bit weary, took the departure as a failure. If only he had known how to find Hocine work, he would have stayed with them, with his wife, with his son to be born in a few months. And nothing was more frustrating than that feeling of being incapable of offering what one wanted so much to offer. Fatiha, standing behind her in-laws, did not cross the threshold; she remained impassive. Yamina, very upset, stood at her side. Hocine waved just before disappearing around the corner. Aïcha cried: "My son!"

Then she quickly went back in, her face full of tears, the little ones still hanging to her skirt. Amor followed her. Fatiha went into her room. Yamina hestitated to follow her; Aïcha called and asked her to come and take care of the little ones. She obeyed.

Fatiha threw herself on the mattress and cried; she cried for being abandoned with a family she did not consider hers, in which she felt foreign; she cried for being condemned to this life she did not accept; she cried for her powerlessness to change anything whatsoever; she cried from these overwhelming emotions, confrontations, and the lack of understanding; she cried for her aborted hopes, disappointed desires, and drifting affections.

III.

Life was difficult for everyone in the days that followed Hocine's departure—heavy with disappointment and resentment, with that feeling of emptiness departures always leave. Amor remained silent, angry with himself for not having been able to make the necessary contacts to get work for his son in order to keep him at home. Aïcha was nervous, wallowing in her sorrow, certain the person really responsible was none other than Fatiha. This created an insufferable atmosphere: she did not speak to her except to tell her what had to be done; she became irritated with everything; even the little ones, who always benefited from her greatest indulgence, were victims of her ill humor and they cried more than usual. Yamina was more discrete than ever, more docile, more conciliatory, as if her only purpose in life was to serve others, lighten the shocks, avoid aggravations. Allaoua found every pretext to get out and avoid the family atmosphere.

Fatiha locked herself in her room every chance she got; she sought peace there, but she was too tormented to find any. One moment looking out the window distracted her, then the next moment it would irritate her: it reminded her that she could not go out, could not take a walk like the young women she so envied who walked past her window. She did not even feel like sewing, nor knitting for the child to be born. The child she unconsciously forbade herself to think about because it would only make her that much more dependent on her new family environment, even though, according to tradition, by becoming a mother, she would acquire new rights. Nevertheless she liked this window on the street, with all the children running back and forth, one-upping each other with ideas for ingenious toys —like the bicycle wheel manipulated with a metal rod to roll it as fast as possible, at times even over the feet of unappreciative passers-by. All these little girls, carefree the way she had been—who would probably be married and locked in like herself shortly after puberty—reminded her of her recent past, her wedding, her present and her future. She liked hearing the music from the record shop next door. Even the horns and noises of the street seemed agreeable from time to time. The old seller of jasmine with the smell that would reach her every now and then: his call was like a chant; and the crazy old man who passed almost every day, now smiling, now angry and quick to insult; and that drunk, everything had become familiar to her and part of her universe. In her spare time she listened to the radio. She loved music enormously, especially the music that made her want to dance. She also listened to the news, which now seemed to be about a world she no longer belonged to, was so far away from. Some programs, some discussions, pointed out even more—if it needed pointing out—her exclusion from anywhere interesting things were happening. . . The speakers gave her the impression of belonging to a society which was not hers. How could the things they debated interest her, since she was destined to remain there, closed in, without being able to participate in social life, without being able to practice the profession she liked? Often there were discussions about women, but not about any of her problems; she could not see how to relate all that was being said to her own life; she did not see anything that could help her to change her life. They often spoke of freedom; but in order to talk about freedom they should be able to hear a woman who yells: I am not free and I want to be free! "I love you freedom, as I love my own son." A woman yelled that during the War of Independence. At that time women could yell it, but today? Today a woman can't go out without a veil because her family forbade it; she can't go out alone because her family forbade it; she can't live alone with her husband because tradition forbade it; she can't work outside of the house because... Fatiha thought and thought about it and she stumbled over the words like a bird bangs against the bars of its cage just after being caught. Her physical discomfort became more frequent each day. She ate less and less.

"You have to force yourself! You have to force yourself for the child!"

Aïcha became alarmed and begain to look for sure-fire remedies. "She could not keep her husband home; she will not be a good mother! Oh, God...what should we do?"

Fatiha was in her room when she saw her friend Myriem pass by in the street; she ran to the front door and opened it wide. The two friends threw themselves into each other's arms. Aïcha saw them and rushed over. Myriem greeted Aïcha.

"Come in, come in..."

Myriem followed Aïcha. Fatiha was irritated. She knew her mother-in-law would not leave them alone. Myriem embraced Yamina and the little ones.

"Have a seat!"

Myriem was about to sit down when Fatiha took her by the arm and led her to her room under the reproachful look of Aïcha.

"Come on, Myriem, come on; I have so many things to show you, all my wedding gifts..."

"Excuse me," Myriem said to Aïcha with a smile.

She followed Fatiha. Yamina understood Fatiha's behavior perfectly; she got up to bring back the little ones who were following them. Aïcha, upset, went out to the courtyard grumbling.

Once the door was closed Fatiha took Myriem's two hands, looked at her, and laughed.

"We were very impolite...but how could we have done it otherwise? She wouldn't have left us alone for a minute! That's the way she is! I'm so happy to see you! Why didn't you come sooner?"

"But I came twice and each time your mother-in-law said you were out with your husband."

"What! I wasn't out...I've only been out once to buy some shoes! A memorable day! Hocine made me wear a veil and follow him the way his grandmother followed his grandfather...I suppose!"

Myriem began to laugh and so did Fatiha.

"I'm laughing because you are here but in fact...I'm furious!"

"I decided to force the door today!"

"Were you worried about me? Excuse me, but I wanted to see you so much."

"Madame Suissi told me to send you her love and Fatma and Khadra too... We talk about you a lot, you know!"

"Thank you, Myriem. Give them my love too. Don't forget...but you know the school seems so far now, so far..."

The two young women remained silent; Myriem looked at her friend and found her changed, different, pale and thinner.

"I'm not happy, Myriem."

Myriem took her hand.

"I'd hoped Hocine, having lived in France, would've been more modern, more open, that we would be able to talk, understand each other, decide our lives together, our children's lives; but no... He follows tradition. Probably so that he doesn't have any problems and because, deep down, he doesn't care; it doesn't bother him... He's gone back to France and left me here... He slapped me for no reason and didn't even apologize for it... From time to time I've had the feeling he could be different, but for that we would have to live in our own house, by ourselves... He's so strange; he talks so little; he changes so much from one moment to the next..."

"How you have changed, Fatiha!"

"Oh, Myriem, don't get married like that! You have to resist it *before* it happens! You don't know what to do any more afterwards!"

"How you have changed!"

"Yes, I have changed a lot! There's this rebellion inside me that I can barely control and my mother-in-law keenly senses it. She has a lot of intuition; she watches me all the time; I worry her, she keeps an eye on her son's wife, the future mother of her grandson! If I listened to her, if I followed her like a mother hen, she would be the most charming woman... You'll see, in a few seconds she's going to come in, I'm sure of it!"

"No mistake about that, we're always being watched! Something happened at school. Djamila and Fatma were walking with Abdou, Djamila's cousin, and Omar, one of his friends. They were stopped by the police and, because they didn't have their papers with them, they were taken to the police station! Can you imagine? Just going for a walk and being suspected of prostitution! It's really incredible! The boys didn't have any problems... they can walk freely, go anywhere, and nobody says anything to them! And you can just imagine their parents! Of course they were beaten. And at the station... they really got an earful."

The door opened and Aïcha came in.

"Come now, the coffee's ready."

Myriem and Fatiha could not help sneaking a glance and a smile to each other.

"We're coming, we're coming...," Fatiha answered calmly. Aïcha went out, and once she was gone Fatiha laughed.

"Leaving us alone for a few minutes is more than she can bear! But you'll come back often, won't you? She'll get used to you. Knock on the window before you come in and I'll come and open the door myself. That way she can't send you off."

"I'll come back, I promise!"

That day the two friends could not have a longer intimacy. While they were promising to see each other as often as possible, Aïcha decided to do everything possible to limit their encounters. She believed Fatiha was not adapted to her new family enough to be able to visit with a childhood friend.

Fatiha did not adapt easily; she noted this with worry, frustration and sadness. Aïcha knew of a few difficult cases, but they had all worked themselves out after a while. She had never imagined that this sort of thing could have happened in her family. They did not really deserve it. Of one thing she was sure: in such a situation, severity was the only effective remedy. Anyway, what woman did not have to adapt, as well as she could, to her new family? She herself had to put up with the unyielding authority of her father-in-law and her mother-in-law's ill humor... That's life! Aïcha considered her own character to be very easygoing and her husband's authority to be just what it should be to keep everything in order. There was no call for dangerous innovations. The happiness of a woman, of a mother, did not depend on it. Happiness... had she found it herself? She did not ask herself the question. She lived, and living is the good and the bad together, the easy and the difficult, illusion and disillusion, love, death. . . Yes, LIVING is all that. . . God be praised. The hardest times were all in the past, those times when each second was full of fear for your loved ones, from injustice, wounds, torture, death. When her heart was too heavy with worry she turned to God, she spoke to him, she prayed to him. But these young people? They seem alone with themselves; they do not know how to pray any more. Aïcha believed that her eldest son's wife had to become a real woman and a real woman had to be just exactly like herself!

Fatiha walked slowly around the courtyard. It was a calm and clear evening. She played with a large veil which she put over her face, took it off, wrapped it like a scarf, waved it. She walked around the fig tree which seemed more mysterious at night. She caressed one of its large leaves. She heard the TV the family was gathered around in the living room. A warm breeze carried the perfume of orange trees and the smell of coffee.

"Why aren't you watching TV with us?"

Aïcha's voice made her jump.

"I need to walk a bit; I need some fresh air."

"Come in!"

"I need to walk a bit; I need some fresh air. . ."

"Come in, I said, you're going to catch cold. You can't think only of yourself!"

Fatiha continued to walk as if her mother-in-law had said nothing. Aïcha went back in grumbling. Fatiha felt the desire to cross the front door and walk alone in the streets. Then, tired of walking in circles all of a sudden, she sat down.

Aïcha came back with the firm determination to make Fatiha come in.

"What are you doing, Fatiha? Really, do you want to get sick by staying out in the night like that?"

Fatiha went to her room without a word.

The silence between the two women was broken only for the minute details of daily life, like cleaning, cooking, washing up, what had to be or did not have to be done.

The next day, towards noon, the postman brought a money order from France. Aïcha rushed over and asked Fatiha to sign.

"Thank you, my son! Thank you!"

She went back to the kitchen with Fatiha to sort chick-peas. The chick-peas. . . There were always chick-peas to sort! Never had Fatiha sorted so many; and while the three of them were there, forced together, Aïcha took advantage of the situation to tell them edifying stories designed to form their young minds. But the money order was on Aïcha's mind.

"Hocine sends money; he's a good son, a good husband. But without a letter! That's strange! Maybe we'll get one tomorrow. Oh. . . why did he leave again? Why do our children have to go into exile like this?"

Fatiha left in a single bound, unable any longer to bear her mother-in-law's laments and the connotations she gave them. She dropped the chick-peas and did not even pick them up.

"What a person! What a person! Oh, we really made a mistake. Life isn't going to be easy. Yamina, I don't want you to copy Fatiha, do you hear? Pick up the chick-peas! Oh, if only Hocine had stayed!"

But Fatiha believed that if Hocine had stayed things would be just the same.

That night, alone in her room, she thought nothing could change her life. She could not even recognize herself any more; she had been a talkative person, yet now she remained quiet; she had never had an outburst of temper, yet now she was on edge all day long. Before she had such a joy for life, now she had no taste for anything. Even the child growing within her did not preoccupy her, but rather the boredom, the anguish, the loneliness—and rebellion; a rebellion she felt without really understanding and to which she could see no end. She felt dizzy and out of breath; she lay on her bed completely dressed and fell asleep with all the lights on. Half an hour later she was woken up by Aïcha.

"What do you mean going to bed like that! And what about the lights?"

She turned her back.

"Really, we've got to watch her all the time! My son, my son, when you come back, I swear you'll find a real wife!"

Fatiha, still very sleepy, lay back again and fell asleep. The next morning as soon as Aïcha saw her she said, "Fatiha, you left your lights on! You're behaving like a child!"

Fatiha looked at her but said nothing; she tried to remember what had happened the evening before but everything was blurred for the moment. And what difference did it make anyway?

Allaoua, eating the breakfast served by his mother and young sister, smiled at Fatiha; their eyes crossed but Fatiha did not smile—she seemed to be somewhere else. He felt a great deal of sympathy for her and felt badly that she was not happy with them. He would have liked to find the means to change things; but things do not change easily no matter how strong the desire; he had no idea what to do and his attempts were more awkward than they were useful. Perhaps it was more than sympathy he felt towards his young sister-in-law. Physically, he had intense desires for a woman, and he was attracted to Fatiha, whose own body had barely been awakened to sexual life. Her maladjustment to it let one suppose that there might be other aspirations. Nor did the sadness in her eyes lack charm . . . But he considered her a sister, and any thought which did not correspond to a brother-sister relationship was buried deep in his mind, rejected, rerouted. Without a doubt, all of this underlay his strong desire to help Fatiha and his continual challenge to everything that was imposed on her. What was imposed on his sister, Yamina, provoked less rebellion within him, and he allowed himself to be served according to tradition. . . and not without pleasure. . . From time to time he dreamt he was a superman, capable of resolving everything and, within a few minutes, could construct the perfect 'James Bond' scenario. . . but reality left little room for the usefulness of such dreams. He would have to come back to the real dimensions of his life, disappointed.

"What sort of film is this to be showing on TV on a Thursday evening! Yamina, you should put the children to bed; they're dead on their feet. It's not even interesting!"

Yamina, used to obeying her mother, reluctantly left the TV, very carefully picked up the sleeping little Ali and then came back for Néfissa.

"I think this film is very good." Allaoua said this just to protest as there was nothing so great about this American film.

"Of course you would! I would have been surprised otherwise!"

Amor looked at his son, trying to guess the real reason for his enthusiasm, if there really was any. . . .

"Why, 'of course'? I don't like all films. . ."

Amor got up and left the room. "TV is destroying you and you don't even realize it!"

Aïcha, strengthened by her husband's backing, turned off the TV and left the living room as well. Allaoua turned the TV back on with a laugh. He looked at Fatiha who had remained seated in the same place as if nothing had happened.

"This film isn't really so good; you can guess everything before it happens; life isn't so simple!"

"No, life isn't so simple."

Fatiha smiled at Allaoua; she was grateful to him for being there, for being different, for being able to protest.

"A movie whiles away the time, it changes things a little; even when it's not so good it makes you think about certain things; it's all so different from our lives; sometimes it makes you dream . . . and when you're locked in like I am . . ."

"Who turned the TV back on?" Aïcha asked, rushing back into the room.

"I did. We can at least watch the film until the end, can't we? If they show it on TV it's so we can watch it, right?"

Unable to have any effect on her son, Aïcha turned towards Fatiha.

"Fatiha, it's late; go to bed. Tomorrow you'll complain of being tired again!"

Fatiha got up and left without a word.

"She could at least watch a film until the end!"

"Mind your own business!"

"Mind your own business . . ."

His older brother had told him the same thing. "Yes . . . but what is my business exactly? What is our business?" he wondered. He got up and left the room. Aïcha turned off the TV again, then the lights, and went to join her husband in their room. Once Allaoua was sure that his mother was in her room, he knocked lightly on Fatiha's door; she opened the door a crack and was surprised to see her young brother-in-law.

"Fatiha, I've got some books and some newspapers if you'd like, would you?"

"Oh, yes! But not tonight; tomorrow, Allaoua, and it would be better if your mother didn't find out."

"I know, I know. Don't worry, she won't find out.

Good night."
He left furtively.

Shortly after that, Fatiha offered to teach her young sister-in-law to read and write, secretly, since Aïcha would be against it. Yamina accepted. She wanted so much to know how to read and write, but was afraid of displeasing her mother. Fatiha promised the utmost vigilance, and Allaoua, who shared in the secret, promised to help. They began immediately and Yamina applied herself to such an extent and with so much enthusiasm, that she progressed very rapidly. At the same time their friendship grew and dared to express itself more openly.

"I wish I could have gone to school like you did."

"As you can see it hasn't been much use!"

"Oh, yes it has! Everything is so different when you know how to read and write..."

Fatiha thought Yamina was right. Everything was so different. Now that Allaoua was secretly bringing her books and newspapers, she was a bit less oppressed by the life she was leading.

"You will learn how to read!"

"Do you think so?"

"Of course, you can see for yourself, you're learning very fast."

They organized their little conspiracy; it was decided to mask the reading and writing with sewing lessons, since Fatiha could teach Yamina everything she had learned herself. Aïcha wanted Fatiha to teach her daughter what she knew about sewing, because sewing was indispensable and the more you know in this field the better... but she wanted to protect her from Fatiha's influence just as much;

all of this was obviously a complete contradiction, but with her usual good sense, Aïcha did not allow herself to be trapped by contradictions she could not handle. She accepted the sewing sessions, promising to participate as often as possible. So the lessons officially began.

All of this, this new complicity between her and Allaoua, this stronger friendship with her young sister-in-law, this game of cat and mouse with Aïcha, made the days a bit less monotonous, a bit less empty, and Fatiha enjoyed it. It was not the knowledge of reading and writing that Aïcha opposed, but rather, the consequences this knowledge had on women. Fatiha now understood perfectly the arbitrary relations of cause and effect that her mother-in-law so firmly believed in and from which nothing, it seemed, could dissuade her. Her every act, all of her authority, even her anguish and anger concerned only her intense desire to keep the family on the path of the ways and customs proven through the ages.

"My mother always says that school makes girls conceited and unbearable!"

"Your mother doesn't really want to understand anything! Fortunately all the women of her generation aren't like her!"

They laughed and the clandestine lesson continued; as soon as they heard the slightest suspicious noise they hurriedly put the books, paper and pens away and took out some material, a needle and thread; the sewing hid the prohibited lessons perfectly.

Allaoua had brought them some beginner's books and Yamina went straight to the task, she practiced every chance she got, there was a bit of pride in her haste; she liked Fatiha's compliments and her brother's encouragements, but she liked this mental work she had been denied even more, she got completely new pleasures out of it, and looked forward to even greater ones. The slight worries, stemming from the fear of displeasing her mother, stemming from this disobedience, which was so new, weren't without their own pleasure as well. All of these contradictory sentiments and impressions, bringing her into a more complex universe, did not displease her.

Allaoua, reading a newspaper, crossed paths with his father. Amor tapped his son tenderly on the cheek.

"So. . . we lost again? Four to one! Not very glorious!" He laughed.

"Well, what do you expect. . ."

"It was written!"

Allaoua laughed and watched his father go out. He wondered if he had said that humorously or seriously. He didn't really know what to think of what was written or not written. . . but he could not understand at all how things like what work a man did, or what he wanted, were written . . . It was brain-racking! Not for his father, of course, who always seemed to be perfectly "informed" about the divine "writings." Then Hocine's departure. . . was it also "written"? And that he, Allaoua, did not agree. . . was this also "written"? Aïcha interrupted his meditations on freedom.

"You're going to waste your time again filling your head with useless things. . . and we know what that leads to!"

Allaoua, who was quite happy, laughed and waited for his mother to disappear so that he could give the newspaper and the book he had promised to Fatiha. He knocked on the door and entered furtively. Fatiha and his sister were lying on the bed. Yamina had her ear on Fatiha's stomach; they were both smiling and it was rare to see Fatiha smile. . . this smile contrasted with her increasingly pale and drawn face. Yamina sat up.

"I heard him! I heard him! He moved!"

She clapped her hands, got up and danced a step. A boy, a girl? A boy? A girl? She hummed, then, suddenly, she saw the surprised and marveling Allaoua at the door. She stopped in her tracks. Fatiha, who had been watching her and laughing, turned her eyes towards the door that she had not heard open and Allaoua, immobile, at the threshold of the mystery of woman, was moved almost to tears. Fatiha quickly took the newspaper and the book that he had brought.

"Go away quickly, Allaoua! If your mother found the three of us here! Go quickly and thank you!"

She smiled at him. Allaoua left quickly, less from the fear of his mother than from this inexplicable and agreeable feeling within him.

With all the work to be done in the house, the mornings passed quickly but the afternoons were often long. When her mother had invited friends to the house it was a real party for Fatiha and her brothers and sisters. Fatiha had known them since her early childhood and it was an occasion to eat a bit more cake. But here, with her in-laws, while these receptions might fill up the time, Fatiha never enjoyed herself. Aïcha adored these friendly afternoon receptions, these small parties for women; she forgot her troubles by chatting about everything and nothing; everything satisfied her, from the interminable greetings to the more or less good news about everybody and everything. Women hold the secrets of perfumes, adornment, futilities, light and scoffing laughter, and other secrets as well, deep complicity, solidarity, intense affectionate participation, in life, in love, in death, in all dramas; they also have malice, jealousy, meanness, superstitions that were not only feminine but were exacerbated by this traditional life within limited space, with its specific openings and closings to the world. Aïcha followed closely, and she was not the only one, the latest episode in the life of Mr. X or Mrs. Y that was told by one of the other and always with the true talent of an actress. What is the use of knowing how to read when one can tell stories so well! Life does not only happen in books. . . it is narrated. . . One of her old friends, Taos, was more of a gossiper than a narrator, but you could not do without her. She knew everything and what she did not know. . . maybe she made it up! Each week's gossip was expected from her. The latest adventures of the butcher's widow, who was only interested in herself; the latest news of El Mekki's son, who had just found a good job in a state company and was looking for a wife; the news of Bonghaba's daughter, who had refused to marry and was locked in by her father and brothers, along with the latest misdoings of Si Ahmed's eldest, who had no sooner gotten out of prison for robbery than he almost stabbed somebody to death last week, another boy as bad as he was! In such peaceful lives that believed themselves protected from misfortune, these things are told. They come from outside, they live outside, and they frighten. But God be praised that they are not in our homes! Taos—this was the way she wished to be called in spite of the great deal of respect they showed her, commensurate with her omniscience—knew everything in the life of the neighborhood, thanks to her circle of informers; but she also knew the good of the blue powders, the benefits of snakes, iguanas, and toads cut into pieces, prepared and soaked like it was done in the old days. It was said she could heal illnesses and bring erring husbands back home. The women who believed came to her for various care, spells, witchcraft, and those who did not believe, pretended they did in order to avoid problems. Taos enjoyed her powers and, at times, the unhealthy fear they inspired. Aïcha knew "it was better to be on her right side than on her wrong side" and acted accordingly. But Fatiha did not take the safe road of listening, of docility; she found this woman quite unbearable and sometimes she even hated her, especially when her look became piercing, her stature even more authoritarian, more self-assured, with her evil and dangerous talk. It was Taos whom Aïcha asked for a remedy to bring back Fatiha's appetite and color and to make the baby beautiful. Taos made a mixture so nauseating that Fatiha threw it away with the dirty water. Aïcha preferred to ignore this so that Taos would not find out, as she too feared her, although they had known each other since childhood. But the devil of a woman seemed to have guessed.

"Are you sure your daughter-in-law took the potion? I doubt it. . . if she had taken it she would have a better complexion. . . it is unfailing. . . my friend, your daughter-in-law is difficult!. . . You'd better keep an eye on her!"

Taos had noticed that Fatiha often vanished and almost never participated in the fun of these afternoons; she even felt Fatiha tried to escape her and she hastened to confide in Aïcha who had no other solution than to make Fatiha have more respect and common decency.

It was when Fatiha saw the way Yamina enjoyed these afternoon breaks in the monotony of family life, that she remembered how she herself got great pleasure from her mother's friends at these coffee hours: where feminine friendship, tenderness, and gaiety were openly manifested; where it seemed good to be together out of the man's world, sometimes so hard and imperative. Those gatherings had not prefigured her whole life to come! Unlike her mother-in-law's friends today, those gatherings didn't force her to ponder with such acuity and distress the semicloistered life of women; time that closed in on itself—when she wanted so much an outlet for an active life, one not completely decided in advance, a life which was part of modern times and not one of the past. She saw in these women here the image of what she would be in ten years, twenty years, thirty years. . . if everything went the way her mother- and father-in-law and her husband had decided. She rejected this image of her future life with all her might. More than once she had left these women's gatherings, not because she didn't like the women, but because her thoughts, feelings, rejections, provoked a nausea in her. Her throat tightened until she could no longer swallow anything at all, that oppression, that dizziness, those tears that sometimes drown everything.

At night, after one of Aïcha's receptions, Fatiha discovered the sensitivity of her body, of her sex, and experienced the pleasure that Hocine had not known how—or had not been able—to give her. The caresses soothed and loosened her throat. She fell asleep. In the morning she was calm. Once she remembered her discovery and her pleasure she was certain that it must be a forbidden pleasure, for no one had ever spoken to her about this. All day these barely discovered and as yet not understood pleasures linked up in her thoughts with certain caresses of women at the baths, their laughter, their looks. She thought of Hocine's enjoyment. He did not love her, but he had experienced great physical pleasure while her own body had been wounded and brutalized. It was not fair. If a man's body can get pleasure then a woman's body has to be able to as well. Yes, everything could be different. She had some inkling of different relationships between men and women than those that were imposed on her; she aspired to other kinds of tenderness. To her rejection of her present life were added new desires, new demands, new calls.

Aïcha and Amor listened attentively and happily as Allaoua read a letter from Hocine; he deciphered it with difficulty.

"Fortunately it's not long, it's a monkey's handwriting!"

The remark displeased Aïcha. Ali lifted his nose, looking at Allaoua:

"It's not true, it's not true! Monkeys can't write!"

"Then you're a monkey too . . . you don't know how to write!"

Always moved by whatever his youngest son said,

Amor hugged him affectionately. "Listen like a good boy, dear, it's a letter from your big brother."

Ali was playing with the dibs, held tightly for fear that Néfissa would take them.

Yamina called Fatiha: "Fatiha! Fatiha! Come here, there's a letter from Hocine."

Allaoua continued reading.

"I am well in spite of the never ending cold. My love to you all; I think of you all very much. Take good care of yourselves!"

Fatiha came in just in time to hear the last sentences. Aïcha had already taken the letter and held it to her heart.

"Your husband is well," Amor said softly to Fatiha. "He hopes you are well too; he is looking forward to the good news!"

"Thank you."

Fatiha looked at her father-in-law, Aïcha, then Allaoua, and turned away.

"Here's a letter from her husband, good news, and that's all the effect it has on her! What's the matter with her? I'll never understand her!"

Amor turned the TV on as if to create a diversion; the screen lit up and folk dancers from the south appeared.

"The matter. . . the matter. . . is that she would like to read the letter from her husband herself; she would like him to write to her directly; she knows how to read; she is his wife. . ."

Now Amor was irritated and turned towards Allaoua: "Allaoua, please!"

Allaoua left the living room followed by Yamina, and Aïcha began complaining.

"What is happening to this house? What is happening?"

Ali came and sat on his father's lap to watch TV.

"Hey, papa, is it true monkeys know how to write?"

"Monkeys like you, yes!"

"I'm not a monkey!"

Amor hugged his son again.

"Write... write... what for? The children don't respect you any more! And if she thinks I don't know she's secretly teaching Yamina how to read instead of how to make dresses, she's mistaken! But this is going to stop; I'm going to separate them; she is too bad of an influence!"

"Stop exaggerating. It's not serious. Nowadays writing is a good thing to know. When the child's born everything will fall into place!"

"It's always the same with you; you can't see it coming and when it happens, then a big fit of rage! But then it's too late... oh, you men..."

"Please, Aïcha, if you would only stop dramatizing things, everything would go better."

"Now say it's my fault!"

"I'm only saying it's all a question of temperament and that it's not really important."

"We'll see... we'll see all right. Ah! Who would've thought...

She swallowed the rest of her sentence and Amor began smoking while half watching the TV with the child who had just fallen asleep on his lap. Néfissa was dead on her feet and Yamina had put her to bed, then stayed in her room to avoid any new disputes.

That night Fatiha felt ill. She woke with a start; her stomach hurt and she was out of breath; she yelled. Aïcha was not sleeping and came quickly.

"What's the matter, my daughter? Don't worry, it's nothing..."

She neared and saw Fatiha's contracted face, her paleness, and her distraught stare.

"It's nothing, my daughter! May God be with us! May he keep the evil spirits away!"

She began walking around the bed continuing her invocation. Fatiha went on moaning and Aïcha suddenly stopped. At that moment Amor came into the room.

"I want my parents; it hurts terribly! I want to see my parents."

"Tomorrow we'll call a doctor and we'll tell your parents to come," Amor said.

Aïcha was irritated not to have been left alone to take care of Fatiha. She felt compelled to minimize the seriousness of Fatiha's condition and of her own anxiety.

"It's nothing. These things happen in her condition. I'm going to make some herb tea. Don't worry."

Fatiha tossed and turned; she was suffering from pain and apprehension; she felt a weight on her breast preventing her from breathing. Aïcha softly backed out of the room while Amor stayed near Fatiha, who seemed to be dozing off now. He quietly left the room and went to wake Yamina, asking her to stay with her sister-in-law.

"Watch over her; if there's anything wrong, come and wake us up right away."

Yamina quickly put on a robe; when she reached Fatiha she found her asleep. Aïcha came in with the herb tea.

"What are you doing here?"

"Father asked me to spend the night with Fatiha."

"She's already asleep; it's nothing. These things happen in her condition! But if Father asked you to stay, then stay; if she wakes up reheat the tea, it will do her good. Tomorrow we'll go get a midwife. We women always have something wrong with us..."

She left vexed and worried. Yamina watched her sister-in-law, her friend, sleep. Fatiha's expression seemed painful, as if she had had a nightmare; Yamina caressed her hair, wiped the sweat from her forehead very gently so as not to wake her; she kissed her and seeing Fatiha did not waken, she lay down alongside her and remained awake for quite a while, her imagination drifting, fed by her apprehension. She could see Fatiha very ill, Hocine coming back from France and crying. Then, she fell asleep.

The following day Fatiha was not awakened until very late by the voices of her parents, who were there around her, lifting her into their arms, kissing her.

The pain had not gone.

"I don't want to stay here any more, take me away!"

"But, my child, be reasonable, you're married! You're going to have a baby; your place is here. You felt ill. Don't worry, my dear, this happens in your condition. A doctor is coming."

"I'm suffocating here, I'm suffocating!"

She seemed to be suffocating for real; she brought her hand to her throat; she felt worse and worse. She had put hope in her parents; there was nothing more they could do for her. She was suffocating . . .

Fatiha was taken to the hospital.

Before leaving, Kaddour confided in Amor:

"She doesn't seem to be adjusting. Her husband has left. She is young. We're worried!"

"I thought Hocine would stay. I did everything I could to get him to stay with us; but he didn't find any work here; I wanted to help him; but it wasn't easy for him; he preferred to go away again for a while. . ."

"This is not good! I didn't think things would work out like this! We're worried! She's changed so much! Today's young women are different; they don't react like our wives; they've been to school; it's difficult, I know . . ."

They had separated, deep in thought, anxious and perplexed.

At the hospital, they passed a very young woman on the stairs. She was in tears, being insulted and pushed around by three angry men.

Fatiha stared at her intently. She was very tired and climbed the steps with difficulty. Her stomach still hurt; a nurse showed them to a waiting room full of people. Houria only looked at her daughter, her paleness, the signs of suffering and worry; Kaddour looked at the floor; he began to pray. Fatiha, almost glad to be anywhere else than in her in-law's house, seemed to breathe easier.

At the end of the consultation, which Fatiha found very difficult, the doctor said:

"We have to hospitalize her and run a series of tests; I can't tell you any more now." As he left, he told the nurse, "It could be a miscarriage."

He said it in a low voice, but not low enough for the others to ignore. Houria looked at Fatiha uneasily. Fatiha showed no reaction; she was surprised by the discovery of the endless hallways, rooms, entrance formalities, rolling beds, the sick moaning, the wounded arriving in Emergency, bloody. She was discovering this universe of bottles, syringes, medicine; this universe with illness and anguish at its center. Fatiha, overwhelmed, felt sick again.

Her first visit, after her mother's, was from Myriem, who had been notified by Houria. She brought flowers, candy, and an international fashion magazine.

"It's great! Wait till you see this!"

"Shh! My neighbor was operated on only two days ago."

"What's the matter with her?"

"I don't know."

"And you, what's the matter with you?"

"I don't know. My stomach hurt badly; I felt ill. They started doing tests this morning."

"Don't worry; they won't find anything wrong! Does your husband know?"

"Oh, no! They probably won't let him know. Anyway, it's better that way, what difference would it make? You know, I can't even write to him; I don't have his address and he only writes to his parents; it's as if I didn't exist!"

Myriem touched her friend's stomach and smiled.

"This one doesn't have any problems yet!"

Fatiha laughed. She began thumbing through the fashion catalogue.

"Look. . . they imitate our traditional styles in Europe! It's quite beautiful! Can you imagine us in dresses like that?"

They broke out in laughter, forgetting about the person who had been operated on, then remembering, began speaking softly again. Myriem took a book from her bag, then a second and handed them to Fatiha.

"That one's a beautiful love novel. . . a story like a dream!"

"Oh, you musn't dream too much. I, myself, I want to live, I don't want to dream life away!"

For a moment, she was suprised with what she had said, intuitively perceiving that it had much greater significance than she grasped, but Myriem went on:

"This one was written by a Palestinian nurse. You'll see, it's very hard to read but it's a must."

Fatiha hid the books under her mattress while thanking Myriem.

"You're hiding them?"

"I'd better! You never know with my mother-in-law and I prefer to avoid a scene."

"If she's anything like my mother, all the better if they don't know how to read; they're so unwilling to change!"

They were happy to be together again, eat candy, laugh, and admire the tulips that were already opening.

"I'll read all of it! Thank you! It's so incredible, I almost don't dare to say it. . . but to you. . . I can tell you anything. . . I'm almost happy to be here, not to be sick, of course! But to be somewhere else than at my in-laws'. Myriem, what is going to become of me? I don't think I'll ever get used to it."

Myriem looked at her friend, so much thinner, so different from before and her face so pale; she was worried but hid her feelings.

"Don't think about it; don't torment yourself. You're tired now; you have to take care of yourself, that's the most important thing; afterwards. . ."

The woman in the next bed turned and moaned. Myriem and Fatiha looked at her and fell quiet. Myriem thought it was terrible to be next to someone who was suffering and groaning; that Fatiha would rather be there made her understand how distressed she was. She knew Fatiha was hiding a lot from her out of modesty, and she regretted these restrictions on what they could share, for the moment insurmountable. She was sorry she couldn't help her change her life. It was this powerlessness that hurt her and made her indignant.

When they parted, Fatiha watched Myriem leave and felt a surge of affection; she liked Myriem's softness, her delicacy, sensitivity, her joy, her exuberant taste for life, which made her enjoy things so much, at times even a bit greedy, curious and jealous; she found her even more beautiful than before; she envied her; she now perceived everything that made their lives different and which would increase the silence between them.

Fatiha was tired and dozed off for a few minutes. When she woke up, Aïcha was leaning over her bed smiling at her.

"You scared us, my daughter, but thanks to God, the child is doing well and you already look better. I trust you are eating? You have to eat well, my daughter; you have to feed him well!"

Fatiha smiled at Aïcha; she knew this kindness was intended more for the future mother than for herself, but this didn't bother her. She understood her mother-in-law's anticipation, which was so much greater than her own; if she told her mother-in-law that, when she had heard the word miscarriage, she didn't even care, Aïcha would look at her as if she was a monster! Was she a monster? Why was she, at times, so intensely aware of this life within her womb, this future birth, and at other times so detached? It wasn't without some surprise and worry that she realized the extent to which one could experience contradictory impressions and sentiments.

"Who brought you these flowers?"

"My friend Myriem, she left just before you got here."

Aïcha remembered Myriem perfectly, and also her desire to separate her from Fatiha, but she pretended to have forgotten.

"Myriem? Is that Mehiddine's and Warda's daughter; the one who came to the house?"

"Yes."

"She's the same age as you, isn't she? Is she getting married soon?"

"She's still going to school."

"School... that's not what makes a woman!"

Fatiha smiled. Aïcha's persistant and tireless reaffirmation of her personal convictons amused Fatiha now that she was not at the house.

"It seems you're going to be able to come back home soon, once they've finished the tests; that's what the doctor said. I was sure nothing was the matter with you... but nowadays they do all sorts of tests! Here... I brought you some oranges, they're good for you, and some cookies, too."

Fatiha thanked Aïcha. Aïcha refused to see her daughter-in-law's sickly appearance. Fatiha's roommate was watching Aïcha and, once she had left, she said:

"Is that your mother, my dear?"

"No, my mother-in-law."

"She looks like a good woman. Oh! In our time we weren't cared for like today! I had eight children, I lost three at birth and one in the war. I was married when I was fifteen but I never had anything to complain about, he was a good man. Is this your first child?"

Fatiha nodded.

"It will be a son! There have to be daughters too, of course, but the first one, we always expect a boy! A· beautiful boy, you'll see!"

She turned to doze again—the operation had tired her so—and when she slept she forgot her fear, her suffering.

A boy? A girl? What difference does it make? Fatiha stopped herself from thinking any more about the child to be born. The marriage. . .the first birth. . .the second. . .life with her in-laws. Caught in the gears. Too many certainties that her future would be the way she did not want it to be. Too many uncertainties felt in confusion. She only needed to let herself think about this future for her breathing to become shorter and the weight on her breast heavier. So, she stared at the top of the palm tree outside her window and, from time to time, her thoughts drifted with the rhythm of its swaying; or she would read a book or the fashion magazine that had so many ideas about things to do.

Fatiha's stay was extended, as they still feared a miscarriage and some tests had to be continued. Her illness had brought renewed visits from her family, her friends, and a completely different Aïcha than the one at home—which surprised her a bit even though she did not let herself believe in future miracles. The circumstances were different, that's all!

Her most intense experiences here were her new relationships, already almost friendships, with a few, and the discovery of a world she had been completely unaware of. The hospital, frightening and attracting her at the same time, suddenly opened all the doors to another universe; the new faces; the novel adventures others recounted; the benign or total suffering of the body, but also of hearts, of souls. The hospital was women's lives, difficult, exposed, no longer hidden; it was the fatigue of successive births; it was lassitude; it was a hundred novels that would never be written, only told or whispered over the hours; it was regrets, hopes that dared to be expressed. The hospital was also the fear inspired in her by the doctors, who ruled as absolute masters like parents in a family. They provoked and expected respect for their knowledge, for their powers. Her stay here helped her to understand her perpetual situation of dependence. Dependence at the house; dependence at the hospital; constraints there, constraints here; obedience; she had been reduced to obedience; the others knew what was good for her. "It's for your own good, my daughter!" She had nothing to say about it; nobody asked her what she thought. The others knew. The more she evaluated her own ignorance, the more she detested it. At times she wondered if she would be capable of being a nurse, to be so daily at the service of the sick, open to suffering, to death. It had never occurred to her that she could be a doctor. There was only one young woman doctor on the ward and she was a doctor's daughter. It had never occurred to her that if she had wanted to become a seamstress it was only because she knew about that profession, and knew very little about all the others now becoming available to women.

Here, she had understood it.

She came to understand that her studies, which she was not even able to finish, were possible and acceptable to her family, because her technical school was well regarded. She discovered with surprise that what she thought was her greatest liberty was not such a great liberty at all. This stay became an awakening; everything that happened, everything that she learned, enriched, clarified her own life; she also discovered power relations more violent than those she had known, and everything they missed out on: tenderness, solidarity, hope.

Four women came frequently to chat with her.
Leila, a twenty-two year old school teacher, was lively,

enthusiastic, congenial, with an honest gaze and a nice smile. Her liveliness was infectious. She had just been operated on and was already feeling well; just a little more rest and she would go back to work. Her work was not exactly restful, but she liked it tremendously.

Zahra, who had just celebrated her thirtieth birthday, worked in a chemical factory and was in the hospital under observation for anemia and blood poisoning, most likely caused by her work; she was looking forward to leaving the hospital; her husband and two children were impatient for her to come home. Worried and silent, she liked keeping company with Leila, the optimist, and followed her everywhere.

Fatouma was only sixteen years old; she was a high school student and had just been operated on for appendicitis, but she still had a fever which prevented her from leaving. She walked around with her transistor radio glued to her ear and commented out loud on all the social and political news. She liked Fatiha very much—one of those spontaneous attractions that are hard to explain. Also, they were almost the same age and Fatiha knew how to listen so well. Fatouma needed so much to say out loud what she liked and did not like, what she wanted and did not want, her plans, her ideas, her taste for everything modern and her scorn for everything that was old.

Noura was over fifty; she had just had a kidney operation and Leila had secretly confided to Fatiha that she probably had cancer, but was not aware of it. She had had six children; her husband washed cars in a garage and she did house cleaning. Noura was very happy with these four women, so different from herself, so friendly, so open. She had never been able to speak so freely. The hospital, with these encounters, removed from family and work situations, this time in parentheses, made possible certain discussions which would not have taken place elsewhere. They talked together until they were tired, but it was a pleasant fatigue. Without them she would have been quite alone since she received no visits; her family was in the country and it was difficult for them to come to the city.

"I don't understand you young people; you're always talking about going to work, but me, with six children, I would've liked to have gone without house cleaning jobs!"

"But house cleaning is not going to work!" Fatouma quickly answered to Noura.

"Oh! Doing house cleaning is not going to work? I'd like to see you do it. You'd see if it wasn't work!"

"That's not what I meant to say, excuse me! Of course it's work and it's tiring, but when we women say we want to work, it means we don't just want to do house cleaning!"

They laughed at Fatouma's confusion as she tried unsuccessfully to get out of her *faux pas*.

"You don't want to do house cleaning; but the house has got to be cleaned! You can't live in filth!"

Noura asked Fatiha:

"You learned how to sew, right?"

"Yes, but I was married off, I didn't finish. . ."

"You certainly know enough for your needs. Knowing how to sew is useful! Do you know how to make dresses? I've always wanted a blue dress in the latest style! It will be a while before I'll be able to afford one."

Fatouma came back, with her usual spirit, delighted to exonerate herself:

"Fatiha will make you one, won't you, Fatiha?"

"I don't know if I can; I had another two years to go! I would really have liked to finish and to have gotten a job."

"Get a job! And me who would be so happy with nothing to do!"

"And are you happy with your husband and your parents-in-law, Fatiha?" Zahra asked.

"My husband. . .he's gone back to France; he doesn't want me to work; it was his parents who wanted him to marry; we didn't know each other and I think he would have wanted a wife like his mother..."

Leila and Zahra broke out in laughter. Fatouma remained serious and attentive.

"I'm not surprised," Zahra said, "you know men, they have been so spoiled by their mothers! I try not to do the same thing with my sons, but it's hard! I've got three men...who all want to be waited on!"

"That's life," Noura said to Zahra, who was beginning to express herself more openly with her new friends.

"Do all four of you live together?" Fatiha asked.

"Yes, all four of us."

"That's better, I think."

"Me," said Fatouma as vehemently as always, "I want to choose my husband, choose my work, decide my life for myself!"

"Is that all!" Noura answered, stupefied by Fatouma's categorical tone, which she herself would have never dared to use, and especially at that age! True, they were not from the same milieu!

"When you want something you have to fight for it, that's what life's about! I'll marry a man who understands that."

"And you think such a man's been born," Leila exclaimed while laughing. "Me," she continued, "I was supposed to marry my cousin Ali; we knew each other and we liked each other; he didn't want me to work, neither did his parents for that matter, but I wanted to be a school teacher; I didn't want to stay at home and live the way my mother had lived...so..."

"So?" asked Noura.

"So...I'm single! I'm a school teacher, but I'm single! And if my mother hadn't supported me I wouldn't even have been able to be a school teacher!"

"What about your cousin?" Zahra asked.

"Oh, he got married to a more docile woman."

"He didn't love you!" Fatouma said.

"Yes, he loved me, it's more complicated than that!"

She laughed, but her laughter hid a trace of bitterness and her friends were not fooled. Fatiha felt sympathy for her, even tenderness.

"You really wanted to get married?" Fatouma asked. She always wanted to follow things through to the end, not always knowing where they would lead.

"Yes, I wanted to get married, have children and work in my profession. But men who agree to their wives working and accept them as equals are not the most numerous! I think they're frightened . . ."

They fell quiet, and in the silence a thousand and one thoughts jumbled together. They would be very difficult to express. At the end of this silence Noura said very softly:

"But, my children, it's life that is hard, we don't often do what we want to in life . . ."

"For us women, it's difficult," Zahra said, as if she were talking to herself; "it's difficult at work, it's difficult with the husband, with the family; sometimes it's so difficult, so hard, that we become discouraged!"

"Can't you understand it's life that's hard . . ." Noura repeated, still following her train of thought.

Fatiha and Leila felt very said as they knew she probably would not be cured; they wanted to know, in a strange communion of thought, if there hadn't been, in the face of great suffering in her life, small and great happiness, great bolts of joy; or whether she was on earth just to transmit life and leave, duty accomplished, painfully. She spoke very little of her children, though it seemed a couple had made something of themselves, as they say. They did not seem very present to her. But she did speak with love of Bachir, her youngest son; he loved his parents the way they were; he even seemed to understand his father when he came home a bit drunk; if he believed in God he would be perfect . . . but he never practices his religion. May God forgive him. . . but he doesn't do anything wrong. Someone told her that he was involved in politics but she didn't know. He is a good son. . . If they had had the money, he would have been a scholar, since he is very intelligent, but they didn't have the money. . . so. . . .

Fatouma, who hated anything that looked like surrender, broke the silence.

"If you think like that then you let anything happen. As for me, I don't want to let things happen. . . and at the high school we promised each other. . ."

"Oh! the promises of youth! But what happens to it all in life?" Noura said. "You don't want to believe that life is like rapids. It carries you away."

"I don't want to be carried away by the rapids. I want to love, to be loved. . ."

"Like in the song!" Noura said laughing. "You know love, it passes! And when it's gone, so what? Besides, the women who are free are no happier for it! Life is really complicated and you are still too young to understand."

"You, you've put up with everything. Well, for us, no! No, no and no! What my brother is permitted to do I will do too! I get beatings and I do it again!"

"You're right," Leila said with a laugh, "but avoid getting knocked out just the same!"

She thought that if there were many Fatoumas, perhaps things would change more quickly. . .

"You frighten me, my children, you frighten me. Life is so complicated, unless it's simple, very simple, much simpler than we believe. Maybe we're the ones complicating life? Anyway, everything changes so quickly nowadays, we can't follow any more. . . we get lost, we get lost. . ."

The conversations, interrupted by medical treatment and hospital rules, began once more a few hours later or the next day, just as if they had never ceased, with two, three, four, or all five of them. Everything was touched on: illnesses, the hospital, a song, a story told by one or the other, but Fatouma, being a young "feminist" and delighted to have new women friends of different ages, pursued her favorite subject with insistence and perseverence. She had just learned that a young girl had died recently from the beating her father and her brothers had given her because a "stupid doctor had declared she was not a virgin! And what was done about it? Nothing! I hear that at the high school they drew up a leaflet; but it was confiscated! And to top it all off, the doctor was wrong!"

"A mistake or not, it's horrible!" Zahra said.

"As long as women are treated like that there won't be any socialism," Leila said.

"When I arrived here, at the hospital," Fatiha said, recalling the striking scene she had witnessed, "I saw a young woman crying, with three men insulting her and pushing her around."

"If only we would help each other more, us women; if only we would rebel a bit more. . ."

"The way you go on, Fatouma!" Zahra said, always surprised by her vehemence and combativeness. "You know, at the factory, there're people who speak a little bit like you but things don't change any faster for it. I noticed. . . that when passions are running high, when everybody is outraged, that's when things move forward. But then again, sometimes it's only a grass fire, it flares up but only leaves ashes and the heat goes away!"

" 'Algeria is a country in the middle of revolution,' some of my colleagues at school say. 'You have to be patient and resolve the problems one by one. After Independence there was enormous progress for us; at last we could get into school, go to university.' All of that's true; but most women who've been to school go back to the old life when they get married, like their mothers, and that is what's bad, and those who don't, come up against so much social pressure. . ."

146

"Are you trying to say we'll never get out of this rut?"
Fatouma asked Leila, whose life as a single woman was
very difficult in this world where women had no right to be
unmarried. "So, tradition will always be the strongest?"

"No, of course not; that's not what I'm saying. I'm
saying it's still too strong, and if we try to fight it we have a
hard life, and a lot of sisters can't struggle against it. If you
knew how impossible it is to live as a single woman
without all sorts of gossip following you... When I got my
first post in a high school just outside Algiers, sometimes I
wanted to go for a walk by myself at night, to the sea, it did
me a lot of good after a day's work; well, people found fault
with that and shortly thereafter I was always followed by a
police car: to watch me? to protect me? The children's
parents invented incredible stories; it's thanks to my pupils
that things were finally cleared up; they got to know me, to
accept me, but you need to be so patient! And the least
mistake can be fatal. It's very hard. Mentalities change
very, very slowly..."

"But do you think we're doing everything we have to
so that things can change?"

A nurse crossed the room holding the arm of a woman
who seemed not to have control of all her faculties. She saw
the five women sitting together and signalled them to
leave.

"Can one go crazy because they're unhappy? Do you
think so?" Fatouma asked seriously.

"Of course, my daughter, of course... you suffer, and
you suffer... and then, one day, you break!"

They fell silent a moment.

"My mother," Leila said deep in thought, "she found
the solution: to keep all her energy, she takes it out on
others! I have to admit that she's really been through it!
Married at sixteen, poverty, eleven children, death, the war,
and my father beat her. Just the same he was not a mean
man. I've only realized that recently. We hurt each other

without wanting to."

"That's the truth," Zahra said. "I told that to my husband one day and he cried."

"We want so much for life to be different, but how to go about it?" Noura took Fatouma's hand with affection.

"My daughter, there's a lot of truth in what you say, sometimes, but you are too fiery, too much in a hurry; it takes time for things to happen..."

Fatiha liked Noura's beautiful face, so attentive, so deep, and she felt a great tenderness for her. Ah, if only her mother-in-law had been a woman like that! She felt such a thrust of affection for these four women who came to talk to her that she practically had tears in her eyes.

"Here we talk, we listen to each other, we try to understand, it does a lot of good; with my parents-in-law it's been months since I've been able to talk."

The four women looked warmly at Fatiha and smiled at her; they too thought it was good to be able to talk to each other, to try to understand each other, to comprehend, to be able to talk freely, without family or other constraints...

"We've got so much more to say to each other, we'll have to work it out so we can stay here for a while!" Fatouma said and broke out in laughter.

"And we have to promise to stay friends, after..."

"Promised!" Leila, Zahra and Fatiha said spontaneously and laughed.

"Ah, these young people! Always making oaths! But life... But, all the same, if we could stay friends it would be nice..." Fatouma gave Noura a quick kiss on the cheek, then turned to Fatiha:

"I've got some things to show you, stuff we pass around the high school."

"You're in high school to work, not to pass stuff around!"

Noura had imitated Fatouma and the five women

broke out in laughter.

"You young people, you think you can change everything, but life... it's like the earth; for it to be good to us, it takes work, time and prayers..."

And Zahra thought: "Ah... if praying could change things... but there have been mountains of prayers and..."

The nurse came back.

"What are you all still doing here? I told you to go back to your places! A little bit is all right, but you go too far. You know very well that the doctors don't like it!"

"Oh, we're just talking a little, to pass the time, it keeps up our morale!"

"Let's go, let's go..."

She motioned the women off, and as they nonchalantly left, she said to Fatouma:

"Oh, you, you know you still have a temperature; you have to rest and not excite yourself talking so much; you talk too much; that's what gives you a temperature! And you won't leave here until you don't have any temperature!"

Fatouma left and winked to Fatiha, who smiled at her, sitting happily on her bed.

Fatiha liked Zahra very much. She seemed to have an intense spiritual life, was persistent, and stuck to her decisions. She did not ask for the impossible, but wanted to achieve everything that was possible. She and her husband worked in the same factory.

"Your wife, she wants to dominate you and you know that's no good!" Everyone knows that anyone who has been dominated cannot try to free themselves without immediately being accused of wanting in turn to dominate someone else, as if it were impossible to establish other relationships between men and women, for example between male workers, female workers and foremen... He had wanted a divorce... but they were still together; she had succeeded, with a great deal of patience, in changing the way they related to each other. Their marriage had been arranged according to tradition, but affection developed between them: the union of their hearts and bodies was good. They still had many problems... but who doesn't? Zahra systematically rejected confrontations and arguments. She preferred perseverence and determination. "You don't pick fruit before it's ripe," she said. Fatiha believed that if Zahra had been able to achieve that, it was because she lived alone with her husband; their respective families were far away in the country; it was because they both worked... What could Zahra have done in her situation? Fatiha would have liked to speak with Zahra at length about her life, about Hocine, love, and sex, but they had to become more intimate first. And at that moment Zahra was so worried about her health! She had brought Fatiha a book about children saying she "could take it when she left and anyway, they would see each other again," and Fatiha had answered "yes," as if she were free to choose her relationships and her friends.

"You'll see how interesting it is. Here I have time to read... When I get home I don't know when I'll find the time... with my three men! But I'll find some, because you can discover everything by reading, everything... You can read things they don't have on television or on the radio! I'm going on and on... it's all because I'm afraid. I'm so afraid that I'll be sick for a long time! I've done so much to try and get on top of this, I musn't be sick for a long time, do you understand? They're in no hurry to carry out tests... So, I have to wait... always wait... As if I had the time to wait... and the money! I hope it's not because of my work that I'm sick, I need to work... I'm sorry, Fatiha, I go on and on... today, I feel so down!"

Zahra returned to her bed, a bit flustered at having confided her fear to Fatiha, but Fatiha had such a nice smile;

she felt so much friendship for her, because she was so discreet, so full of hopes, so sensitive, and obviously so unsatisfied, so unhappy . . . She wished she could help her . . . but how? It seemed to her, unless some break was made, that Fatiha's situation was hopeless, and that the only advice you could give in such a situation would entail grave consequences. Zahra knew well from experience how difficult it was for a woman in their society to break away from tradition, if she is not helped by her family or by exceptional and favorable circumstances. She understood clearly that one whould not provoke recklessness nor irreversible and dead end moves. The risks of losing everything were too great. You had to try everything that was possible, but not go too far, to avoid getting smashed . . . Fatiha was also thinking about the distance between what was possible and their goals, and she wondered: "What is possible for me? For Hocine and me? For the three of us?" Then she thought of Zahra again. "I only hope her illness is curable!"

Fatouma interrupted her thinking; she brought her some leaflets that one of her friends had just given her that were put out at her high school.

"Hey, look, they went on strike!"

"On strike?"

"Yes, they wanted an end to the medical inspections."

"Medical inspections?"

"Yes, medical controls of our virginity! They are obsessed with our virginity! As if that was the most important thing! Especially when they want us to lose it in the end!"

She laughed and Fatiha did too.

"They also went on strike to support striking women workers. You can imagine the rest! Like Noura says: 'You're in high school to learn and not to go on strike!' "

She laughed again. The nurse walked by.

"You, there again?"

Fatouma left quickly, because that was the third time the nurse had warned her. Fatiha watched her go. She knew

Fatouma would turn around and smile with a mischievous wink, as usual. They were about the same age, but what different lives they led! Fatiha liked Fatouma's attractive, lively, intelligent personality, and she spoke about everything with so much daring! As for Fatouma, she did not dislike being able to proselytize n this way, without any difficulty, it must be said, since all of this was completely new for Fatiha and she had hardly any definite ideas about the topics Fatouma brought up with such self-confidence, a bit of a premature self-confidence according to Leila and Zahra, but quite appealing nonetheless.

Fatiha read through the leaflet Fatouma had left her:

"For a real democratic status. As Algerian women, we think it is up to us women to defend our rights and to take charge of our struggle so that a real democratie status for Algerian women is instituted . . ."

Fatiha's attention had already waned. These words, these sentences, did not make sufficiently concrete sense for her to really understand. Nothing had prepared her for this political language, for this militant solidarity of women against everything she saw as so firmly established, for this women's struggle, for the formulation of women's aspirations as women. *"We denounce . . . We demand . . . a real judicial and social status guaranteeing women their rights, freedoms, their legitimate aspirations, for a real woman's divorce and the free choice of partners."* Yes . . . free choice . . . it was necessary . . . *"To abolish the law."* She did not understand this very well and she told herself she would have to speak to Leila and Fatouma about it. *"For the abolition of parental and marital tutelage" . . .* "Tutelage?" In fact, it sounded like, but said in another way, what her family had not respected—her desire to continue her studies and get married to a person she loved; and what her new family paid absolutely no attention to—her desire to live with her husband and decide their lives with him. Yes, that she understood; but the terms seemed so abstract that it was almost impossible for her to relate them to her own personal experience and to all the emotion and even passion that she felt. She put the leaflet down on her bed. If she had been to high school like Fatouma she would understand better. And what would she have done afterwards? University? To study what? It was so far out of the realm of possibility for her family that she was not even able to ask herself what she would have liked to have done. What about Fatouma? She wanted to study pharmacology; because she liked it? Or because her father was a pharmacist? And what happens if she gets thrown out of the high school? Noura said they would marry her off. Fatouma had told Fatiha about the influence her brother Kader, two years older than her, had on their father, but her father was partial to her because she wanted to take the same studies he had, while his son aimed for a career in business administration and had grandiose ambitions, because, as everyone knows, business administration opens all the doors. Kader showed a certain progressiveness in words towards women, but he exercised a vigilant authority over his sister. He claimed the right to forbid her to go out to cafés to have tea with her friends, to go out by herself after her classes, and a lot of other things. He watched over her virginity as if it were the family treasure; the confrontations between them were violent; he even slapped her sometimes; he urged his parents to marry her off as quickly as possible. Could she resist for much longer? Would her parents continue their firm support for her? If not, what would happen to all her plans and defiance? Fatiha recalled all the tragic stories Aïcha had told to scare them, her and Yamina, and to turn them away from the slightest desire for independence. The big family house was the protective place *par excellence*; evil stopped at its door. The most frightening specter was prostitution, the ultimate downfall, the pit of dishonor. But how did one become a prostitute? Aïcha's only answer was: the woman who does not follow tradition is lost! "They say that in the Casbah, men pass before doors protected by bars; women offer themselves, their breasts exposed. An old matron, with cakes of make-up, covered in jewelry, guards the door and makes the clients pay!" Woman-talk at the baths, curious, ill at ease, a bit ashamed to have spoken about it. Here, when she asked the question, the women had not laughed; they were not ill at ease, not ashamed; they had spoken about prostitution seriously.

Zahra, Noura, Leila and Fatouma spoke very seriously about things in life. Fatiha began to realize that she had been kept away from a knowledge of reality, and she wanted to know what was real. Why would this ignorance be cultivated, if not to keep her more docile, more submissive? More protected too, perhaps. Reality surely seemed to be full of secret pieces, complicated and often hostile. They had hidden life from her, they had even lied to her, and now she felt the deep need to struggle against lies and deceit. It was difficult to talk about everything freely; it was as if one was always afraid, afraid to ask questions, afraid to confide in anyone, afraid to cross doors, afraid to do what one wanted to do with all one's heart. She was afraid too. But her fear was not as strong as her desire to know about life, as her confidence in life, as her appetite for happiness. She felt very close to her friends, who did not hide the risks, but didn't turn them into paralyzing terror, either.

Leila had told her the story of Baya; she did not know the story of Baya; she did not know the painting of Baya; she did not know that, as a young orphan, she was placed with a French painter, then she had begun to paint. Aïcha did not tell the story of Baya, neither had anybody in her family. A great art gallery in Paris had exhibited her paintings in 1947 when she was sixteen years old. André Breton, a famous French poet, prefaced her catalogue; it was an immense success. She went to an art school in Vallauris, France, and met Picasso, and then nobody heard talk of

Baya any more... She became the second wife of a man who had initially asked for her hand for his son. She had six children and never painted again, except at an odd moment here and there. In 1963 she was rediscovered by Algiers and proclaimed a 'great artist,' but nobody ever saw her; she came incognito to her expositions, veiled, accompanied, protected... Baya, woman painter, cloistered... Baya, isolated... How can such things still happen today? Fatiha felt the urge to become acquainted with the paintings of Baya and Picasso. An orphan who had been placed as a house cleaner became a famous artist! A woman can become an artist of fame... a woman can dance, sing, write, fly a plane... a woman can do anything... Then she began imagining that she was working material and she enjoyed it very much.

Fatiha was still supposed to remain in bed to avoid a miscarriage but she was getting up more often and for longer periods of time; she had gained weight, regained some color and appetite. She did whatever she could for those around her but did not feel that she was cut out to be a nurse; she wouldn't like to spend her life in a hospital. Too much suffering. There was only one woman doctor and she almost never saw her; a few women lab technicians; Fatiha felt sorry for them, she wouldn't like to face all those test tubes and analyze sick people's blood. But she surprised herself by thinking of these professions, as if she still had a choice to make.

She attentively read the newspapers Fatouma brought her, and was pleased to be able to read them peacefully without having to hide them. She used all her strength to push away the recognition that the prohibitions and petty connivance were soon to begin again.

She cut out an article about emigrant workers. "Men At A Discount." It was a terrible title. "These men, denied the simple right to live, forgotten by the laws of the country, poorly paid, badly housed, exposed to police brutality and the racism of those nostalgic for colonialism, it is they who produce a great part of the wealth of France, West Germany and Switzerland." She read this article over and over again, conscious that Hocine was one of those men. The memories flooded back: all the most intense moments of emotion, quarrels, misunderstandings and the unexpected. She saw him walking into their room the night of the wedding, she saw him with his mother under the fig tree, their mutual understanding and tenderness. She relived the moment when she was slapped; she remembered his body on hers . . .

Meanwhile Hocine remained distant; he provoked so many contradictory sentiments within her that she became lost. She heard his voice the evening before he left. "You can't understand." That was certainly her dominant impression, she did not understand. She did not understand and she wanted to understand. She wanted to understand everything: her defiance, her desires, her body, her heart, her life; she wanted to understand Hocine and understand herself, what she had to do to change her life. It created a great urge within her, a great call, and the desire to open wide all the doors of the houses they wanted to shut her up in. Then she thought of the child to be born. She carried him but he was still a stranger, except for those rare moments where a unity seemed to be in the making, unbeknown to her, through the body and heart, and her spirit quieted.

Fatiha only had a few days remaining in the hospital. She decided to write to Hocine but she had no success. One after the other, she tore up all her attempts. She remembered him as so inaccessible, elusive, authoritarian; at times vulnerable yet always so secret. Often she imagined him the way she would have wished him to be, different; they hold hands, talk to each other, desire each other; she is free to go out without a veil, to work; but reality froze her dreams with one stroke, and she tore up the unfinished, unfinishable letter.

Fatouma left the hospital, leaving her address and, with her warm, affectionate smile, the promise of a faithful friendship. Zahra was transferred to another ward. Her blood had been poisoned by chemical products, as Noura simply said, and it would take a long time; she had had a moment of deep depression and now, with her usual determination, she concentrated all her force on doing what she was told to do in order to be cured. To be cured! She wanted to be cured and for that she had no other means than to follow blindly what was demanded of her here. She had had no other option than to work in the only factory near her home that hired women. She had not chosen her job assignment. . . That is what Leila told Fatiha when they were walking for the last time in the hospital yard. Leila left the hospital that same night and Fatiha the next day.

"We want our freedom, but usually life disposes of us as it will, and without our being able to change it . . ."

And Fatiha thought: "When will we walk together again?"

Noura was operated on again; her state was critical; they were deeply saddened. Noura accepted her illness with resignation, as she had accepted everything in her life, and death approached, slowly; there was no escape.

Fatiha and Leila were walking in the hospital yard, arm in arm. They were friends and saw this friendship as something marvelous that somehow they had to find a way to preserve.

They passed women who seemed to be learning how to walk again, with difficulty, careful of their steps. On a bench two women, one young, the other old, seemed to have abandoned reality for delirium. Not far from them, young girls were dancing; one of them had transformed a pot into a percussion instrument and was beating a rhythm for the steps. The two of them drew near and began clapping their hands to the beat.

IV.

It was Houria and Allaoua who came to get Fatiha at the hospital and took her home by taxi while Aïcha and Yamina prepared a good meal to welcome them.

"Everything's all right now, my dear! Everything's all right!"Houria repeated this reassuring sentence several times while kissing her daughter, happy to see her cured, rested, heavier, and God be praised, the child had been saved!

Allaoua, who had come to visit Fatiha only once at the hospital, found her changed. He had stopped and looked at her for a few seconds, smiling. He thought she seemed healthier, but above all, she looked less sad, and there was a spark in her eyes that he enjoyed seeing.

Fatiha did not talk in the taxi. She looked at the city drenched in sunshine, animated, noisy, attractive. For a moment she had the impression she was discovering it again after a long voyage, as if she had come from somewhere else; she felt like walking among all those people who seemed to be going somewhere, that had something to do; and she felt an emptiness within her. She was going to her parents-in-law's and the house she had almost forgotten; she had to make an effort to put the pieces back together again; it seemed strange and almost worrisome. "Everything's all right, my dear. Everything's all right!" Her mother's voice was reassuring. In the streets, women hurried along, bent under the weight of baskets full of vegetables, fruit, clothes, followed by laughing mischievous children, full of energy. Large posters were inviting people to an evening of folk dancing from the south. Men called out to young girls who ignored them. The city. . .

Fatiha was no longer looking; she thought only of returning to her parents-in-law's house, of the days to come. She wished they would be different but she already felt mired in that unalterable daily life preserved by Aïcha.

"Here we are, my dear, here we are. . ."

Allaoua had been observing his young sister-in-law in the rear view mirror for a while; within the space of a few seconds her face contracted, her eyes lost the sparkle they had had earlier, they seemed to be turned towards disturbing images within her, and he understood that Fatiha was not happy to be coming back, and this hurt him; it was as if Fatiha directly transmitted her anguish, her uneasiness, to him.

Aïcha was at the doorstep waiting, as she had awaited her son; Yamina ran, along with the little ones who threw themselves around Fatiha's neck.

Then the party began, warm and spontaneous. Their imaginations ran a bit wild. Aïcha was certain, as was Houria, that everything would be different now that Fatiha had become a real woman, able to live her new life, able to become a mother; the future appeared calm to them, planned in advance, happy, in the image of this moment. As if by magic, Aïcha had forgotten all the past conflicts, and she felt good. She no longer felt any resentment against Fatiha's mother, and the two women chatted about everything and nothing, laughing, eating cakes, drinking coffee, delighted. As for Yamina, she was so overjoyed at Fatiha's return that she laughed from sheer happiness and confided in secret that she had worked well and made a lot of progress. Fatiha really tried to be there at the party but was so only in appearance. She saw reality as it was, without illusions. Nothing had changed. Nothing would change. She would have to teach Yamina secretly; she would have to wear the veil; she would have to stay locked in. . . Nothing would change, not unless she wanted it with all her might, and not unless she found, within herself, the energy and the means to change things; but how? Fatiha once more found herself in this house where she had not been happy, and she knew that Aïcha's joy would not last for long, since the cause of their conflicts had not magically disappeared. They lingered on. Fatiha felt different but not in the way her mother-in-law had hoped. In fact she came back from the hospital enriched by new people, by new friendships, by new knowledge, even less capable of leading the life that had been mapped out for her.

Allaoua did not stick around; as he left he had made a friendly sign to Fatiha, a sign of complicity which meant: "I have some things for you," and Fatiha had smiled to him.

Houria had left; happy, reassured, promising to come back soon and, in the euphoria of the moment, Aïcha had acquiesced with all her heart.

The whole day had been brightened by the party and in the evening, coming home from work, Amor walked into a harmonious, relaxed, gay atmosphere, and found Fatiha transformed, more beautiful, daring to look at him straight on. He gave her a long hug and Fatiha understood that he was already hugging his future grandson, for he wanted a grandson, his first grandchild could only be a son.

They went to bed early and, in bed, where he spoke freely with his wife, Amor uttered the same sentence that

Houria had repeated several times:

"Everything's all right, now. Everything's all right!"

And Aïcha agreed, satisfied.

The uneasiness that Fatiha felt coming back and that only Allaoua had noticed did not last. In fact Fatiha felt much stronger than before she had left, and the sadness had gone. She thought a lot of her new friends and didn't get discouraged looking for ways to see them again. Something new as well, and far from the least important: she felt like a woman expecting a child. This child to be born was now present. She had accepted him at last. She was looking forward to the birth. And this still blurry future was full of plans for the two of them. It was all this that gave her back the appetite she had had before her marriage, her color, and all the little pleasures of life. Reconciled, she perceived all that much more the distance separating her from her mother-in-law and Hocine, and from what they wanted her to be. She and Hocine were not only two irreconcilable personalities opposing each other; there was more to it: there were different aspirations, different needs, that were fanned by the heartbreaks, the new things emerging, the hopes and hopelessness, the balance and imbalance of time stretched on a rack.

Aïcha, seated beneath the fig tree with the little Ali on her lap, kissed him and hummed.

"My darling, my little man. Who's mama's little man? Who's the most handsome? It's Ali!"

The child kissed her and cuddled up to her.

"And who does this little jewel belong to? This little

jewel that we don't show to the girls:

She touched Ali's sex and laughed; he cuddled up to her again, laughing and squealing.

"Who's a little man like papa?"

At that moment Amor crossed the courtyard on his way to work.

"Don't forget the meat tonight," Aïcha reminded him while saying goodbye.

"We can't eat meat every day; it's too expensive, you know that!"

"I'll make some peas! You were supposed to bring me a Tunisian cloak, weren't you? Mine is in such a state! Si Lakhdar could give you a little credit."

"You know Si Lakhdar gives me nothing on credit, he gives credit to nobody for that matter, that's why he's rich! You know he watches everything down to the centimeter. You'll have to wait, wife, we've spent a lot of money lately!"

"Ah! If you had listened to me; if you had been willing . . ."

Amor, impatient, annoyed, and knowing exactly what Aïcha meant, headed towards the door.

"If you had been willing to borrow money from your uncle. He lent some to your brother!"

Amor had already left and Aïcha continued to express herself as if he were still there.

"And now he has a café he doesn't even talk to us any more! He plays the proud one, and us? And his wife, she no longer has the time to come . . ."

The child she was cuddling escaped and ran towards Néfissa to take her ball. Aïcha remained under the fig tree and, as always in those moments, all her feelings raced at a hundred miles an hour, pell-mell: the high cost of living, her worn-out cloak, her husband's lack of ambition, the daily hardships, Hocine in France, the young ones still to bring up, Allaoua, difficult, Fatiha, much better since her return, but would it last? Yamina, soon to be married, all the things tormenting her, all the things she had no real power over. Why was all that coming down on her this morning? She really had no idea. . . . These bad moods would come on her suddenly, she hardly knew why, and they had to be digested or dispersed by little fits of anger, moments of bad mood, tyrannical acts; never taken out on the little ones, almost never on Allaoua, he was a man already. . .

That day Allaoua was charged with accompanying Fatiha and Yamina to the baths. Fatiha thought it was ridiculous to be accompanied in this way, but she offered no resistance; it was not disagreeable to her to go out with Allaoua and Yamina, on the contrary, they got along well together. Besides, it gave them them the chance to talk freely and to consider how Allaoua could act as an intermediary between her and her friends, because there weren't many other solutions. Perhaps they could meet at the baths, but for that things would have to be set up in advance. Allaoua agreed as soon as he was asked. It was decided that he would contact Fatouma first. That was the easiest, since they were the same age and enjoyed the freedom of high school students.

Fatiha liked going to the Turkish baths, and so did Yamina. An atmosphere of happiness and freedom prevailed; conversations were unhampered; family secrets were exchanged without holding back—conflicts over money, the unhappiness of a neglected wife, the extravagances of another, condemned sexual adventures; but none of these shared secrets made them melancholy: the environment of the Turkish bath did not allow for it, it was a place of relaxation, of corporeal pleasure, of laughter, of chatting and tattling. The complicity that reigned here was quite different from that which she had discovered at the hospital. What she -heard at the Turkish baths hardly challenged the ways and customs of the old days and traditional life; the women gossiped about each other in order not to speak too much of themselves. They avoided the essential, to concentrate on the trivial. If they could only deal more with reality, women's lives would change faster. It was this quality of the relationships at the hospital that had surprised Fatiha, and she loved it, it responded to her most heartfelt needs. Was it because the hospital was a place of suffering, of fear, of unanswered questions?

She noticed a woman, about forty, pregnant, who seemed oppressed by the heat and steam. Around her were four, five, six children. . . hers? "A woman who hasn't got five children isn't a woman," Aïcha said time and time again. Fatiha had told Zahra that she did not want any more children.

"Well then, you'll have to go see a doctor and ask for a prescription to take the pill. He'll explain it to you. You'll have to take one every day and never forget, because if you do, you could find yourself with twins!"

They had laughed. But how could she go see a doctor for that? And it seemed that some of them refused to prescribe it unless the husband was present. Did the women around her know of the existence of the pill? Did they refuse it? Were they frightened? Was it their husbands, their families, that refused? Fatiha thought how she would have liked to ask them all these questions. There were women who conducted inquiries for one reason or another. Aïcha had thrown one out of the house, not long before, outraged, although it was not these sorts of questions she had asked, but simple questions about education.

When they left the Turkish baths Allaoua was waiting impatiently, leaning against the wall.

"Hey, you three, you were in no hurry!"

The girls laughed.

"What do you mean, us three?"

Allaoua pointed to Fatiha's stomach.

"He must've been hot!"

"Why 'he'? Perhaps it's a 'she'!"

"It's in your interests to have a boy. That's what mother and father are expecting!"

"I know...I know...but it'll be what it'll be, as for me, I have no preference."

Allaoua had said it only to provoke her, but Fatiha was in a very good mood.

"O.K. now, follow me. You must obey me!"

And he began walking at a fast pace.

"But," said Yamina, "that's not the way home!"

"You must obey me; you haven't got the right to speak!"

He laughed and the two young women looked at him in surprise.

"So what's the matter? Who told you we were going to the house?"

"So then, where are we going?" Yamina asked, more and more suprised. They stopped and Allaoua was forced to do the same.

"It's a surprise! Come on...come on..."

They hesitated, look at each other confused, without moving.

"Come on...come on...We're going to the movies."

"To the movies! You're crazy! If your mother and father ever found out...can you imagine?"

Allaoua shrugged his shoulders as if he did not care. Yamina was worried:

"Let's go home, Allaoua, it'd be better!"

"Come on...let's go! We're going to the movies. It's not the end of the world."

He began to walk. Fatiha and Yamina decided to follow. He was walking briskly, obviously very pleased with himself.

"It's a good film, isn't it? Because if it isn't, it's not worth the hassle."

"Yes...You'll see. They say it's a very good film."

166

He took them to see an Italian film strongly recommended by his friends: *The Old Lady's Money*.

They sat in the last row of the balcony. Fatiha and Yamina hid their faces behind their veils, surrounded by families, couples, single men. They were barely seated when the film began. Fatiha and Yamina, immediately drawn into the film, forgot their escapade. Filled with emotion and anguish they followed the adventures of these poor Italians, trapped by gambling and a monstrously rich American woman who made them gasp, mad with desire, next to the piles of dollars which she would never permit them to win.

Leaving the movie, Allaoua was on a real high. "What a film!"

"What a horrible woman!" Yamina said. "She tormented those poor guys, letting them think they'd make millions. It's monstrous! Do you think such a thing could really happen? My stomach was in knots during the whole film!"

Allaoua laughed, then, thoughtful:

"I don't know if a billionaire like that can really exist! But what really exists is the misery of the Italian people!"

"Gambling...it's an illusion," Fatiha said. "You can't get out of your misery with illusions."

Allaoua, surprised by his sister-in-law's firm tone of voice, turned towards her and said:

"They say that avaricious old billionaire woman, duping the poor, is a truer image of America than its smiling president!"

"I don't understand very well," Yamina said.

"American dollars invade countries but they don't make the people rich."

"It's a complicated film," Fatiha said, "I'd like to see it again; it's nice to go see a good film like that! We should be able to go by ourselves when we feel like it!"

"The suitcase!" Allaoua yelled.

Fatiha laughed. Allaoua had forgotten the suitcase with their things for the bath in the movie and ran back to get them.

"I hope he finds them!"

"Who do you think wants a suitcase with bath things in it?"

Allaoua came running back with the suitcase in his hand.

"Now, let's hurry, and above all shh!"

They laughed and walked towards the house at a steady pace, their minds occupied by different sequences of the film, reflecting on its deeper meaning, recalling forgotten images, happy to have seen an interesting film, happy to have broken the family order. Fatiha wondered how she would be able to go out alone and see a good movie and find her friend Leila, who adored movies. . . But how could she get the money to buy a ticket? As for Allaoua, he was really proud of himself and promised himself to do it again, as often as possible.

Si Lakhdar, elegant, golden jewelry on his fingers, walked with the assurance of those who have a standard of living they are proud of. He looked at women without making advances. Sometimes that worked. The small street peddlers irritated him; sometimes he thought they should all be put in prison—all potential thieves, if they weren't already!—He passed a beggar at a street corner. They should also be forbidden to be on the streets. . .

"Help me. May God help you!"

He already had the help of God! God be praised! And if he had it, it was because he deserved it. Of this, Si Lakhdar was absolutely certain.

A veiled woman handed a coin to the old man who continued to recite his petition; he did not grab it fast enough, his hands were numb; the coin rolled and fell into a hole. It was impossible to get it back out, there was a grill and his hands didn't fit through the bars. The old man contented himself by shaking his head and continued his prayers.

Si Lakhdar was walking behind a pretty woman dressed European style. He hesitated a minute, then took the liberty to talk to her; the young woman did not answer, she did not turn. Si Lakhdar went on his way. Nearing his shop he greeted the neighbors who eagerly greeted him in return. His shop was small but well stocked. When Si Lakhdar entered Amor was coming out of the back room with a piece of material in his hands; two clients were waiting, leaning on the counter. Amor unrolled a couple of meters and the women felt the material, draped it over their shoulders, stood back, approached again, seemed to be considering it intensely.

"This cloth is very good, very good quality."

"Yes, but it's a bit drab."

The woman turned towards her friend, who agreed.

"A bit drab, that's right; we'll think about it; we'll be back tomorrow; you must never rush to buy something; afterwards you're sorry."

They left Amor with a heap of unrolled material, thanked him and left. Si Lakhdar sat at his cash register.

"You mustn't give them the time to think about it, especially at that price!"

"They had come in to look; they didn't feel like buying; that's how they spend their time . . ."

He knew women well . . .

"A good salesman doesn't let that sort of customer leave without buying something."

"But it's the end of the month, Si Lakhdar; the people

don't have much money left; it's the same every month. Towards the end of the month they come to see, the men, too; we roll out a bunch of fabric for nothing!''

"The end of the month or not, you have to sell! There are bills to pay! You have to be forceful. . ."

Amor began putting the material away and didn't answer. Si Lakhdar busied himself with the bills, and then glancing at Amor, blurted:

"I just saw your son."

"Ah!"

"He's a good looking boy now! He was coming out of the movies."

Amor looked at Si Lakhdar and continued putting the fabrics away. Si Lakdhar's tone of voice, which was very familiar, led Amor to suppose that he had something disagreeable to tell him; but what could it be? He really couldn't see any relation between Allaoua at the movies and something disagreeable. Nevertheless, the hypocritical expression on Si Lakhdar's face left no doubt; he was never so amiable as when he was about to say something unkind, something that hurt.

"He goes from time to time, yes. . . the young like the cinema, and he, well, sometimes he likes it a bit too much!"

"He was with two women."

Amor, holding a roll of cloth with outstretched arms stopped, but covered his surprise perfectly.

"With two women? Women or girls? School girls?"

"Women, veiled women."

"Ah!"

Amor continued putting the material away.

"Ah, these young people!" Si Lakhdar said, diving into his accounting once again, more attentive. The telephone rang. Si Lakhdar took the phone off the hook.

"Hello. . . Ah, it's you, Tobni! Yes, yes, it's arrived? No problems with customs? All the better, all the better. Yes. . .

yes. . . I'll come by tonight. Right. Until this evening."

Si Lakhdar hung up.

"Ah, if we don't do something, I won't make ends meet, I won't be able to keep a salesman. . ."

Amor remained quiet and continued putting things away. He knew Si Lakhdar perfectly well, his character, his way of doing things, his small and big deals, and he knew that it was an insurance against unemployment for him; he had developed the habit, in order to keep his job, of being as discreet and secretive as possible; he played the one who saw nothing, heard nothing, and never told anyone anything; as a result, a very particular relationship was established between him and Si Lakhdar, a relationship that did not lack in rerouted aggression. But at that moment it was not Si Lakhdar's deals which preoccupied Amor, but rather Allaoua. Who did he go to the cinema with? Who were these veiled women?

When he got home that night Aïcha was playing with the two little ones in the courtyard, and Allaoua was reading the newspaper under the fig tree. Aïcha immediately perceived that something was wrong.

"Leave us, Aïcha, I have to talk to Allaoua."

Allaoua stood up, surprised by his father's expression. Aïcha went into the house, bringing the little ones whom she entrusted to Yamina, then went back near the door to find out what it was all about.

"Can you tell me what you did this afternoon?"

"This afternoon, I accompanied Yamina and Fatiha to the baths."

"And after that?"

"After that? After. . . I met up with Ali and Saïd to go to the movies."

"Ali and Saïd wear veils and dresses now?"

Amor looked his son straight in the eye.

"I know you were at the movies this afternoon with two

women. It's pointless to lie. So, you go out with worthless women now? Is that how you spend the money I give you?''

Allaoua, stupefied, hesitated, then decided to tell the truth, at once. After all, it was not as bad as that!

"Yes, I was at the movies, but not with worthless women; I was with Fatiha and Yamina.''

Aïcha, standing on the doorstoop, watched and listened, worried.

"What? Say that again!''

"They're shut in all day long; I wanted to entertain them a little; I'm the one who insisted; there's nothing extraordinary about that! Everybody goes to the movies today!''

Amor slapped him with all his might. Allaoua wavered, then straightened up. It took all the respect his father inspired in him not to respond with violence. He stared at his father with defiance, turned and left.

Aïcha came closer, very upset; then she remained fixed in the center of the yard. It was as if she had just received the slap that Allaoua got.

"Because of that woman the father beats his son! Ahhh . . .''

Amor did not look at her as he walked by. He entered the living room, forcing himself to hide that he, too, was deeply upset by the blow he had just given Allaoua, that he was intensely irritated by this transgression of the family order, which he saw as a rebellion.

In an instant all Aïcha's grievances and hostility towards Fatiha flared up again. She had barely returned home, and all the conflicts had started anew, more violent than ever. She was responsible! And Hocine who was not there! . . .

Yamina, who had heard the fight, disappeared after having warned Fatiha. How could father have known about that? Incredible! Who had seen them? Who told him? Their first disobedience sweat blood the first day! And Allaoua had left!

Nobody had dinner that night. Fatiha preferred to stay in her room and nobody came to get her. In the other part of the house she heard the yelling of Aïcha and Yamina who had also been slapped, but by her mother. Amor had asked Aïcha to say nothing to Fatiha because of her condition and her recent return from the hospital. Anyway, as far as Amor was concerned, it was Allaoua's fault and not Fatiha's, and he swore that he would eventually eradicate all these ideas his son had. Yamina and Fatiha had been entrusted to him; it was up to him to make sure the family order was respected! If they felt like going to the movies why hadn't they asked? They would have all gone together. If Hocine were here, and not in France, he would have taken his wife to the movies. Ah. . . that's my son! He had lost his faith, perhaps. . . but not his respect for tradition! He was a good son. Amor began to pray with fervor. "May God help us! May he grant peace in this family again, as he gave peace to the country of our fathers! May he grant that our children stay on the right path! Glory to God! Only he is great enough to convince Hocine to come back. We need him so much. May he be here when his son is born, and may he stay with us, for good!"

Amor punctuated his words by bowing to the ground; then he remained deep in meditation for a long time.

His meditation was disturbed by the yelling of the woman next door; no doubt her husband had come home drunk again, as he did so often, and was beating her. "Alcohol! May God protect us from it!" And he too had just beat his son! Amor began to meditate on violence, on the education of sons, but at no time did it occur to him that he could go speak to Allaoua, speak to Fatiha, to hear what they wished and how they saw the future, because the future was them and not him. His thoughts focused solely on the family order, yet strained towards that future, the future of his children, but as a faithful reproduction of the past; his father had been the protector of this past, and today he was the trustee, and Hocine, once he would get back, would be so in his turn.

Allaoua had already drunk two beers and was ordering a third. He had walked without really knowing where to go and entered the first café he came to. He looked at nothing, saw nothing, heard nothing, not even the music, although it was quite loud; he was engulfed in his bitterness, in his anger for having been slapped by his father just because he had been to the movies with his sister and sister-in-law. It was so ridiculous to have been slapped for that. . . that he would not even dare tell his friends! He swallowed his third beer in one gulp. He was not used to drinking alcohol, and especially beer. He ordered a fourth, as if to completely surrender to this black mood that flooded over him, overwhelmed him.

When he went out he did not feel very good and crossed the street without looking.

"You'd do better to stay on the sidewalk, you donkey! That's how accidents happen."

The taxi driver who had to avoid him accelerated. Such a young man already drunk! What's life coming to? There's not enough authority any more. Allaoua, undecided, returned to the sidewalk and watched the cars and people go by; he could make out some women; his head was spinning a little; he leaned against a tree, then he automatically headed back towards the house. After a while he realized which direction he had taken and stopped in his tracks, rejecting the idea of going home. Radia, a woman the family knew well and who lived about ten minutes from their house, spotted him as she was closing the shutters and saw that he was not well.

"Allaoua!"

"Ah, it's you, Radia?"

"What's the matter? Are you sick? Did you have a fight?"

"I'm not feeling very well."

"Do you want me to take you home?"

"No, I don't want to go home."

"You don't want to go home? You can't stay there, like that, in the middle of the street, the way you look! If you don't want to go home then come in here and rest a minute. Come on, come on. . . ."

Allaoua hesitated, then accepted Radia's offer. He had known her since he was a child. Radia pointed to a couch full of cushions.

"Sit down there; I'm going to make you a very strong coffee, you'll feel better after that."

Allaoua fell into the cushions and was quiet.

"Have you been drinking?"

"Oh, not very much, only a little beer."

"Too much beer, Allaoua!"

"I'm not used to it."

Radia went to the kitchen to prepare the coffee. Allaoua, sunk in the cushions, was half asleep.

"Drink this, it'll make you feel better; come on, drink it while it's hot."

Allaoua took the cup and drank a sip.

"I'm sorry, Radia, I don't want to bother you. But I don't want to go home; I had an argument with my father."

"With your father? You're not going to sleep outside, are you?"

"I don't want to go home."

"Drink your coffee."

Allaoua drank his coffee. He felt better. The strong coffee was already having an effect. Radia looked at him sympathetically; she was beautiful. She sat across from him.

"Is it that bad?" she asked him gently.

Allaoua did not answer.

"Nobody saw you come here; you can stay here, and tomorrow, you'll see, it'll go better; you'll see things a bit more clearly."

"Can I? Do you think? It's not putting you out too much?"

"Of course not, I'm offering it; if you really don't want to go home, it would be better this way. I don't want you to do anything stupid. But your parents are going to be very worried. . .don't you think that. . .''

"I don't want to go home."

"Then, stay here."

"You're very kind."

"Since I've been working, I understand things better."

"What do you do?"

"I'm working at Sonatex, you know, the textile factory."

"Do you like it?"

"It allows me to live, me and my children, without having to ask anybody for anything; it's hard, but I'm independent."

Allaoua looked in the direction of the bedroom for the children. Radia read his mind.

"The children are asleep; they go to bed early; I want them to sleep well so that they can work well at school; you know, for us poor folk, school is the only way to get out of the misery! My oldest is twelve now. She helps me, but I don't want her to be too tired; I want her to succeed, to learn, to have a job that she likes."

Allaoua looked at her in admiration.

"She's lucky to have a mother like you! My mother has always refused to send Yamina to school, and I don't think Néfissa will go either."

"She's wrong. And what do you do?"

"I'm doing a training program in a machine-building workshop. It's interesting."

Radia laughed.

"That's good!"

"This afternoon I took my sister and my sister-in-law to the movies after the bath, and my father found out, I really wonder how! He was furious. He slapped me."

Radia smiled at Allaoua; she did not think that it was all that serious but she didn't want to hurt him any more than he was already.

"Tomorrow, it'll all be forgotten, don't worry...You can even go home now; you're better, and it's not so bad as all that; your parents are going to be very worried..."

"No, no, no! I don't want to go home; that'll teach them to be so closed-minded."

"Do as you wish. You can sleep here on the couch. It's no problem. Tomorrow, you'll have to be very careful of the neighbors; there are so many evil tongues, as they say! We mustn't make it any worse. And we've got to make sure Taos doesn't find out."

She laughed.

"Radia, how could they think that going to the movies dishonors them?"

"Of course there is no dishonor in it, but that's the way they think, and it's very hard to get people to change their way of thinking. It should be possible to get them to understand that women can go to the movies by themselves and still be respectable, but it's difficult, and men, as soon as they see a woman by herself, look down on her and think they can take liberties with her. I gave up going to the movies for that very reason..."

"I know my sister-in-law is not happy; she's bored and my mother doesn't understand her."

"I lived through that. In ten years my husband only came back to the country three times. And with my mother-in-law things did not go so well. And, then, he didn't come back at all; he died over there. It's been three years already! How time flies..."

They became silent.

"When I think he died all by himself over there, it hurts so much."

"We didn't want Hocine to go back, but he couldn't find any work here. And. . . I think he didn't really want to stay, between him and his wife. . . they weren't exactly madly in love! It was an arranged marriage". . .

"People shouldn't be married like that any more, without knowing each other. Young brides shouldn't be shut in with their new families anymore. All that's the past! It doesn't correspond to life today."

"Fatiha wanted to go on with her schooling; she wanted to be a seamstress, work out of the house, go out freely without a veil. . . you are free, you are. . . "

"I left my husband's family so that I could do what I wanted with my children and work. I'm happy to have succeeded at it, and to have found this job. . . "

"It's obvious that you're happy! You are beautiful!"

Radia laughed. They looked at each other with the intentness of two people who discover that they like talking to each other.

"It's true that you look a lot prettier when you like what you are doing. . . but I'm happy about that and I'm sad about other things. . . That's life!"

She heard a child crying and rushed to their room. Allaoua watched her run to her child; he admired her; she came back, he smiled at her.

"He was dreaming, it's nothing! Even children have bad dreams. We want to insulate them from the fear, but you can't."

She sat on the couch. Allaoua felt a strong impulse towards this woman who seemed so human and whose look was affectionate and deep. Radia guessed his impulse towards her and got up.

"Allaoua, it's time to sleep now. Tomorrow, I have to go to work early and the factory is hard. Tomorrow, things will be resolved, you'll see..."

She gave him some covers. He became quiet. The drunkenness passed and left a sort of floating feeling, this woman, kind, calm, understanding... He felt good, good with his awakened desires, good in his body reaching out for a woman's. But the woman escaped again. In Radia's refusal there was no disdain, he was sure of that; there was love, too much love lost to loneliness. Allaoua fell asleep with his warm sex in the palm of his hand. Radia looked at him asleep and went to her room; she looked at the children who were sleeping; she stretched out on the bed, tired from her day of work, from the tensions, the edginess, and her body began to dream of love.

Radia woke Allaoua up before sunrise. Before going home, he went for a walk to be sure that his father had left. Aïcha was hanging the laundry, as if it would lighten her anguish. She heard the door open. "Allaoua!"

"Where have you been? I was worried all night!"

"I was with friends."

"All night?"

"I slept at their place."

"I prepared your things. Go have some breakfast and then go to work; tonight you'll apologize to your father. He doesn't know you didn't come home."

Allaoua took his things for work and left without having breakfast.

Aïcha plopped onto a stool, looked at the laundry yet to be hung, and felt tired. At her age, a whole night of worry with no sleep takes its toll. She resented Allaoua for not having kissed her this morning; she would have liked so much to hold him in her arms. She resented Fatiha, the one responsible. She did not even have the strength to complain with her usual loudness and gesticulations. She no longer knew what to do so that things would go better in the house. Then she had an idea; she left her laundry; she knew Fatiha was in the kitchen and that her work would keep her a while.

A few seconds later Aïcha was in Fatiha's and Hocine's room; she was holding a clay kanoun. The incense smoked and burned on the coal; very slowly and methodically she walked around with the kanoun, the incense filling the whole room. "Blessed be God! Glory to God! I pray You lead these children down the true path; they are young and don't understand Your will anymore; but if You wish it they will achieve wisdom. I pray to You so that peace may come back to this house! Blessed be God! Glory to God!"

Aïcha turned in circles several times in the center of the room. She pronounced inaudible sentences, chasing the evil spirits away. She went towards the wardrobe she had forgotten, opened it wide, let the incense penetrate at length. She became meditative, then closed the door of the wardrobe. The kanoun was no longer smoking; the incense had burned out; the evil spirits had certainly been chased away; so she left slowly, majestically, calm, full of confidence.

She returned to her chores. Fatiha saw her hanging the wash in the courtyard, heavy on the dainty light ankles showing below her Algerian-style trousers. She was surprised to see her so calm, and she feared that under this calm a storm was brewing. She went to her room and was seized by the strong odor of incense. It made her nauseous; she left quickly. She understood and could not help smiling.

All day long, at work, Radia thought of the evening before and of Allaoua. He had awakened her desire; she had felt like making love; and it was very natural: she was a widow, but still young, and she had known the pleasure so little; her husband's visits home had been so rare. Deprived of company, deprived of tenderness, deprived of sex. Loneliness. And the respect she inspired was rooted in these self-imposed frustrations, the loneliness she preserved, simply because she did not want to risk falling into a traditional life again, with its constraints that, today, did more harm than good. She was convinced. Why are the relations between men and women so complicated? Why did the men at the factory, in the streets, behave in a way that expressed such sexual frustration? Radia would like to live differently, but how? Life would be so much more complicated without this respect she preserved with such difficulty.

Fatiha and Yamina were cleaning the living room. Yamina was worried; she listened for the slightest sound.

"Fatiha, you should tell Allaoua to apologize to our father. If he apologizes, we will be forgiven. Allaoua didn't come home last night; if father finds out . . ."

"He didn't come home?"

"Yes, this morning."

"Oh, well. It's not as bad as that, come on, Yamina. What a fuss! As if we shouldn't be able to go to the movies when we feel like it, and to the baths, without a chaperone!"

Yamina looked at her, surprised. She had remained a child, fearful, worried about her parents' will, torn by her completely new desires, her friendship for Fatiha, her affection for her brother, although she did not understand all his ideas and actions. Fatiha had become a woman with more self-assuredness, more self-consciousness. She was no longer the same after her stay at the hospital. The distance between her and Yamina had become greater. And Yamina sensed it without being able to explain it.

"Yamina, there are so many things in life, in the world, more important than that! We're fighting with each other over nothing, really for nothing! We're tiring ourselves out for nothing! It's absurd!"

Yamina did not understand how Fatiha could be so detached from these conflicts that made the family life unbearable. She heard some steps and ran to the other side of the room so that her mother would not find them talking together. Fatiha wondered how she could cure her young sister-in-law of her fears, how she could help her free herself from this hold, how she could get her to understand that all of this was unimportant and that there was so much else to do. Yamina looked out the door and saw her mother put on her veil and go out. She came back over to Fatiha.

"Mother has just gone out."

"Ah! Well, come on, let's work a little..."

"Oh, not today... after everything that's happened..."

"Yes, today, like the other days, if we don't, Yamina, you'll never know how to read and write!"

Fatiha headed towards her room and Yamina followed. Once they got to the bedroom, Fatiha turned on the radio and by chance came across the program: "Youth Have The Mike." Fatiha turned up the volume and signaled to Yamina to come and sit next to her. Yamina breathed in the incense.

"What did you burn in your room? It smells like..."

"It smells like incense...; it was your mother... she exorcised the place and its inhabitants..."

Fatiha laughed, and Yamina opened her eyes wide, full of worry. Fatiha told her to listen.

"To escape a marriage she rejected, a young girl, Sennia, tried to commit suicide by swallowing barbiturates. Fortunately, she was saved in time, and we went to visit her. She had already refused twice to marry; the third time, she ran away, but she was already married. Her father told her: 'You can no longer refuse, you will dishonor the family...' The story of Sennia is not an isolated one; we know of a young office worker who jumped from the fifth floor, and of a young girl who jumped out of the car taking her to her future husband, who is crippled for life as a result. If we speak about these tragic events on the air, it's not because of a taste for the morbid or sensational, it's simply because it's reality; it is not to provoke, it's only to inform. It is so that people can know how far this inflexible respect for tradition can go; it is to support our youth strug-

gling with the difficulties of a world in great change; it is so that we do not veil our faces before such facts; it is so that we arrive at a better understanding of each other, no matter what our age, no matter what social category we come from.''

Fatiha was startled and intrigued by this program she had found by accident. It was the first time she had heard it, and she turned the radio up very loud. Listening attentively, they did not hear Aïcha come in, stunned by what she had just heard and the attention Fatiha and Yamina seemed to be paying to the program. She remained frozen at the threshold, and then, no longer able to hold back, she lunged at the radio, screaming:

"Aren't you ashamed to be listening to such things? Lies! It's scandalous!"

In a fury, she threw the radio on the floor; it ceased to transmit. Aïcha grabbed Yamina by the arm and violently dragged her out of the room.

"I don't ever want to see you in this room again, do you hear, Fatiha? Never!"

And turning towards Fatiha on her way out:

"Hocine will know how you behave! Dear God! Dear God!"

Fatiha, caught by surprise, remained still, then grabbed a cushion and threw it against the wall with all her might, then another, and yet another; she kicked the mattress and began walking back and forth in her room. There seemed to be an uncontrollable multiplication of occurrences designed to set off a chain reaction of new conflicts. This unchecked acceleration of events carried her along against her will. She put her hands on her stomach and felt the baby move. The baby's movement calmed her, as if soliciting a more balanced measure of things. She stood before the mirror and looked at herself; she saw the heaviness of her body; she felt the desire to undo her hair, to let it hang free, to swing it from left to right and from right to left, as if she were running in the wind on the beach. She became aware of the intensity of her look; she smiled at her reflection and her reflection smiled back at her.

The atmosphere had deteriorated very quickly since Fatiha had come back; Aïcha's joy had lasted only a short time. She had to accept the obvious; her daughter-in-law had not changed; she escaped her grasp even more totally than before. Convinced that only firm determination would successfully control this difficult character, Aïcha multiplied the things that were forbidden. She made sure her daughter was with Fatiha as little as possible in order to protect Yamina from her influence, so it became more and more difficult to organize the lessons; but Yamina now had such a desire to continue to learn that she dominated her fears as well as she could and used a great deal of ingenuity, which surprised Fatiha and made her happy.

Aïcha had briefly considered asking Taos for help, but she had preferred to keep her out of her current worries and do without her help, so that the whole neighborhood would not be aware of her problems. That would not have helped things at all. She could have asked her to keep quiet about it, but knowing her very well, her confidence in her promises was quite limited.

Aïcha forbade Fatiha to visit her new friends, persuaded they had a very bad influence on her. She had to be kept away from all these women until the child was born; afterwards, no doubt, and as Amor thought, things would change for the better of themselves. After the child was born, Aïcha thought over and over again to reassure herself, Fatiha would be like all women, tied to the child; she would then have new responsibilities, new powers within the family.

For awhile Aïcha considered telling Hocine, but she had not convinced herself to do it and then again, Amor was against the idea.

As one could expect in such circumstances, Myriem found the door closed and wondered how she could successfully get around the vigilance of Fatiha's mother-in-law. It was obvious she intercepted the letters for her daughter-in-law. In fact, that is just what she did, without a whisper to anybody about it, and since she did not know how to read, nor want anybody to read them, she did not know what they contained, nor who wrote them. As far as Fatiha's parents were concerned, Aïcha preferred not to tell them anything, nor let any of her worry or frustration show; she announced a visit which she ceaselessly put off. In fact there were two letters from Leila, two from Fatouma, one from Zahra, all of whom were concerned not to have heard from her as promised. Fatiha was not fooled. She knew her friends had written; she had warned them of the climate within the family and the authority that weighed down on her; she decided to write and entrust the letters to Allaoua, who would try to contact Fatouma directly as well. She had tried to write to Hocine, but she wrote the letter over and over, tearing up each one; it was so difficult to speak to him simply; they had been together so little and that time had been so tense, so troubled, so unreal; they knew so little of each other; they had so little love for each other; they were so different. . .

The program on the radio that had created a scandal at Hocine's parents' house had set off similar reactions in other families. A few moments after Aïcha had broken the radio, the program was interrupted by order of the station manager, under pressure from the protests that had immediately tied up the switchboard. "Play music!" And the technicians obeyed. As for the producers of the program, although they stormed and raged and argued, nothing they did could get them back on the airwaves. The discussions had been violent.

"Sorry about that, old man, we've been accused of inciting young women to commit suicide!"

" 'The young have the mike,' that's all right but it's no reason to speak about crazy people! There are other things to talk about that are much more important."

"This is an outrage! It's not because you got too many telephone calls that you stopped the program, it's because, for once, we let women speak freely, and because they were getting into subjects that are taboo, or that are supposed be treated the way a select few think they should be treated! You want savagery in the name of tradition to remain secret! Well, I don't go for that! If we can't talk about it, if we can't denounce it, then it means we agree with it, it means we find it completely normal!. . .If we don't speak about it how are we going to change people's mentalities?"

"We can't change them all at once, and women's problems cannot be treated in isolation from the rest!"

"That's exactly what we're doing, we're not isolating it from the rest!"

"There are other ways!"

"They don't seem to be very efficient! How much longer are we going to let our youth commit suicide? There are times when remaining silent is a crime!"

"Don't exaggerate! You can count these suicides on your two hands!"

"You know very well that's not true! And even if there were only a few, that's no reason not to talk about it. Man, you're all a bunch of cowards!"

With that the program's producers, two men and two women, left, slamming the door behind them. And the young women who were to speak about their experiences on the radio left and that was the end of it.

As for Fatiha, she no longer had a radio, and that was extremely painful for her. Allaoua had offered to lend her his while he was out, but Fatiha refused, fearing that it,too, would end up in the garbage.

186

As for Amor, he participated as an impassive spectator in this battle for family order. He felt the women had to settle their problems among themselves. His authority, undisputed, indisputable, watched over things. He was convinced that things would fall into place after the birth; and if an emergency arose, he would write Hocine, so that he could join his son's authority to his own; surely Allaoua would not risk another of these misadventures and Amor thought more and more of Yamina's future. Yamina would have to be married off and Allaoua too; he would have to make irreversible commitments for them as soon as possible. The young were precocious, more independent than they had been; their life was different; parents had to act accordingly; take precautions. When the time came he would speak with his wife.

Fatiha had written to her friends through Allaoua, and as agreed, the answers came through Fatouma and Allaoua; their age, their greater freedoms, made meetings easier. They met and became friends very quickly; both close to Fatiha, both were infatuated with independence and modern life; and since one always enjoys fooling authority and challenging what is forbidden, they multiplied the risks.

Fatiha lacked neither books nor newspapers, but she still lacked independence. A parallel life was organized, but it did not succeed in making daily life acceptable. She felt more and more like a prisoner, and the only way out seemed to be to go to France and join Hocine. Not so much because she wanted to live with him, but because she was his wife and was expecting a child, because it was "leaving" and leaving seemed to hold all the hopes, all the dreams of independence. She was ready, or believed she was, to try anything to no longer live with her parents-in-law, to the drumbeat of tradition. To join Hocine, it was true, remained within the realm of what was permissible. But to accomplish this she would have to write to him.

Every time Fatiha was alone in her room she tried to write a letter to her husband, but it always turned out to be a letter to Leila or an answer to Fatouma or to Zahra.

Zahra was feeling better; it would take another few months for her to get over her anemia from the chemical poisoning, but she would get better and that was the main thing; she would not be able to go back to work at her old job at the factory and that worried her; but she was happy that she had regained her courage, her calm strength, her day-to-day ability to direct her life. Fatiha admired her; she admired Leila too; she often thought of that day when she had said to her friend:

"You're very lucky, Leila; you have a good job and you like it!"

"Yes, it's what I wanted, it's what I do; but you know, there is always a moment where you vacillate, when you don't really know any more where you're at, what you're doing, why, what it is you want exactly, who you are. . . what you want out of life. . . But the next day. . . I see my pupils again; they have such a look, a look that demands everything from me and from the future. . . and I'm off again! . . ."

She remembered that Leila had laughed.

Fatiha felt like seeing her friends again so much, to speak with them, to ask their advice. She did not have any pupils to see again after that moment where one vacillates. . . but she was certain that everybody had the possibility to forge their future, if they want to with all their might. But the letter to Hocine was still not written, every time she started she began to dream instead of writing, and the time passed.

One day she wrote the letter without stopping and did not read it for fear of tearing it up yet another time.

She decided to take it to the post office herself. She crossed the courtyard, veiled. Aïcha suddenly appeared.

"Where are you going?"

"I'm going out, I need to walk. I'm fed up with walking in circles in the courtyard."

"Need to walk! Need to go out! You won't go out alone, that's not done!"

"That wasn't done in the old days, perhaps, but nowadays it is done."

"You won't go out alone, Fatiha; I'm going with you."

She put herself between the door and Fatiha.

"Yamina, bring me my veil."

She blocked the way, and Fatiha waited. Yamina brought her mother's veil. Aïcha wrapped herself in her cloak and went out, followed by Fatiha. Yamina watched them leave and held back the children who ran to follow their mother.

The walk did not last long. Aïcha took advantage of it to buy two or three things she needed, and they went back home without saying a word, and without Fatiha being able to mail her letter.

That night, Fatiha asked Allaoua, who had just brought her a newspaper, to be kind enough to mail the letter to Hocine.

"Ah, finally, you've written!"

"Yes."

"Great! I'll mail it. I promise!"

Allaoua smiled at Fatiha, and as he left winked at her discreetly, the letter to his brother safely in his pocket.

Once the letter had been sent, Fatiha waited for Hocine's answer.

The baby was becoming more and more vigorous, and she felt him moving with more force. At night, in her extreme loneliness, she listened to him, caressed her stomach, thought of their future. And in this tenderness for her body, for life, she found her peace.

In France, Hocine had gotten his job back, but the developing economic crisis intensified the conflicts, and racism was definitely a part of it. You could not go to work any more without reading slogans against immigrant workers, foreigners, Arabs, Blacks on the walls and in the metro. It was rare when a day went by without some reference to oil, as if the dollars of the multinationals or of the oil kings were distributed among the workers. A rare day without mention of unemployment which foreign workers were supposed to be responsible for, and the reminders of the vast *"aid"* France distributed so generously, and that *"would serve industry at home a lot better."* It had become unbearable.

There had been a few official statements on TV. The same people who had fanned the confusion, even provoked it, then tried to explain that nothing was that simple, that a liberal capitalist economy needed foreign workers, meaning: underpaid workers. A worker had been killed while going for a pack of cigarettes, just because he supposedly looked like an Arab; another had been attacked while leaving a dance; another. . . Very rare cases, said the powers that be, and all the worthy citizens who closed their eyes as much as possible to these outrages: to the arson of foreign worker housing and to all those things that came under the official heading of *"unfortunate excesses"*. . . The foreign workers knew that they had to be more vigilant than ever to avoid falling into the traps and provocations which could escalate into tragedy. A draft of a law, adopted by the Council of Ministers and to be discussed by the National Assembly in France, signaled the hour of massive deportations. Two to three hundred thousand expulsions a year were planned. In spite of the official denials foreign workers became scapegoats for an economic situation they were obviously in no way responsible for. They had contributed to the growth and the development of the wealth of France, but had acquired no rights. Indignant voices were raised in the National Assembly:

"Respect for Human Rights begins with the respect of the immigrant works!"

"An xenophobic text!"

"Anti-immigrant text!"

"The workers are being subjected to arbitrariness and insecurity!"

"France, land of expulsions!"

"This text is scandalous, unconstitutional and unacceptable!"

A few demonstrations of solidarity in the streets and in the press. But indignation without the mobilization of public opinion could not block the vote for the draft law. The text was adopted by a parliamentary majority. Another text was to fix the terms of residency and employment for foreigners in France, and institute de facto, a state of permanent insecurity. As soon as there was no work, the authorization to work, as well as the residency permit, could be taken away. During this period of recession a thousand companies a month were closing their doors. . . . Given this situation there was a danger that French workers, frightened by the constantly rising unemployment, would allow themselves to be blinded to the solidarity they should have with these immigrants, who were the most vulnerable and therefore the first victims of those who, basically, have always pitted people against each other in order to maintain their privileges and their domination over the poor, in France and elsewhere.

It was to this world, which had become more difficult and more violent, that Hocine had returned. He had discovered Paris again with a more sensitive and sharpened outlook; he had also found its mystique again, the alluring magic of a very big city. Paris gave him the impression of being able to live two lives at the same time. Back in his country he was now married and would be a father very soon; back in his country were his parents, his brothers, his sisters, his wife... And here, he was single in a way, alone, free. Here, he could hope to improve his situation... In the present circumstances it was an illusion, now more than ever, but nonetheless, even when one refused to dream, he has to hope for the better from time to time, if only to negate the difficulties of the present and the threat of unemployment and deportation. There was also the possibility of an encounter, an encounter with a woman that one never ceases to believe in, as long as one does not have a fulfilling love life. During his stay in Algeria and since his marriage, he had gotten used to the daily presence of a woman; but he did not wish for the presence of Fatiha; he wished for the presence of a real woman at his side, one who liked to make love.

One evening he met two young women; he recognized Françoise; they had slept together last year. For such a short time! They greeted each other. She laughed. She remembered but seemed to be in a hurry.

"How are you?"

"Well, and you?"

"It's been a long time since I last saw you!" She smiled again.

"Excuse me."

She said goodbye to him offhandedly and quickly caught up with her friend. He liked this woman but she obviously no longer wanted anything to do with him... Why? Their lovemaking had been good... She had laughed... They did not argue with each other... That woman was no whore, she did not ask for money; he followed his fantasy... Too bad! It's not easy to find a woman... Hocine thought of Fatiha for a few seconds and then pushed her out of his mind. He did not want his universes to interpenetrate, they were too different; he lived each one separately.

Women... some came to the work site on Friday evenings. A car would stop, toot its horn; two or three women would get out, flaunting themselves. The Spanish workers, talentedly mimicking a corrida as usual, would stop in their tracks, and their Arab and Portuguese spectators would turn around.

"Come on, here we go!"

"Prepare your money!"

"To pay the toll!"

"What's a toll?"

"It's like on the thruway!"

The usual jokes. You have to cover over what's too sordid.

"Come closer. . . so I can wash you."

Off came the trousers, the vest, the shoes stay on. The water sprays on his sex. . . his sex in the hand of a woman. . . It was a woman. . . and her hand was soft.

The women who came to the work site were not alone. . . home delivery. . . that's it! Some guys took the money so that it would go faster, and were a little bit like watchdogs too!

"You're ten francs short! My man, if ya ain't got the bread, borrow some from your pals or work overtime!"

"For this price you can't ask too much! If ya ain't happy, just go to the Champs-Elysées!"

"Hey, you over there! Don't bring her back, eh?"

No. . . that. . . never! Never. . . !

Never. . . not because of those women. . . no. . . because of those guys! Never! It's better to satisfy yourself!

Hocine did not live at the construction site; he shared a room with four friends in one of the rare immigrant hotels that still existed in the fifteenth arrondissement, which had been completely renovated. For a while, he and a friend had nourished the hope of living in one of those big new houses they had built from the ground up. The doors would open automatically to let them in. . . There would be plants in the hall; it would be an apartment with a big living room and a balcony; they would put tapestries everywhere, and there, he would receive a woman, because there, she would feel at ease... With a bathroom all blue like the Mediterranean... One day, with his friend, they began following up the ads and visiting agencies. But they wouldn't even rent a one room studio to two immigrant workers... in the very houses that they built... *maybe* to Arab and African students... but not to manual workers at a construction site... they had occupied the premises previously!... It was a crazy idea anyway... they could not pay such high rents, and live, send money home, save up to nourish their dreams of independence...

Hocine had just received a letter from home and during the lunch break, was looking around the work site for Karim, a young worker who knew how to read and write in French and in Arabic, and with whom he got on well. Karim was talking with a group of workers; but as soon as he saw Hocine he quickly came over.

"I've received a letter, would you read it to me?"

"Of course!"

They sat away from the group of men who were still discussing work, their pay slips, their fears...

"Hocine, my husband,"

Hocine shuddered; the letter was from Fatiha!

"You must know that I was very ill, taken to the hospital, and that the doctors thought I was going to lose the baby! But everything is well for the baby now. And I'm well now too but the doctors said that antagonism was not good for the mother, or the baby. You know I am not happy here. It is probably why I was ill. I cannot go on living like this; I am too bored; I want to come and live with you in

Paris. Write me. Why do you only write to your parents?"

Hocine, taken unawares and deeply angered, quickly grabbed the letter from the young man's hands. He looked at Hocine and then lowered his eyes. Hocine almost crumpled the letter up, then changing his mind, he held the letter our to Karim again, asking him to continue to read.

"Answer me very quickly, Hocine. I hope you are well. I kiss you affectionately. Everyone here is in good health. Your wife, Fatiha."

Hocine took the letter back in anger.

"You look furious. Why? She's your wife!"

"She mustn't write me without telling my parents! She mustn't give me orders!"

"She's not giving you orders; she's confiding in you. What harm is there in that?"

Hocine began smoking nervously.

"And who gave her my address, I wonder; I forbade it! Another one of Allaoua's tricks! Young people back there do whatever pleases them! I'm going to answer, and then we'll see . . ."

"I don't understand you, Hocine, it's a proof of her affection."

"She's liable to show up here! You don't know her! Do you see how we live here! Do you know where I live? I already told her that France was not an ideal place for a worker's wife . . . She's all right back there! What more does she need. She lacks nothing."

"But she's not with you. When you're married, it's to live together, no? It's not to stay alone with your parents-in-law, is it?"

"She's not alone! Me, I have lived for years in these conditions in France, alone. What's more, don't you see the situation today? From one day to the next we can be unemployed, laid off, deported. I didn't want her to come before, much less now! Write what I'm going to dictate to you. If you don't want to write, say so . . ."

195

The young man looked at Hocine and understood that he would not make him change his mind.

"*Dear Parents,*

"*I have just received a letter from Fatiha. You can tell her for me that I know what I have to do, that it is not for her to dictate to me what has to be done . . .*"

He stopped dictating. Karim looked up at him.

"Are you going to send that?"

"Of course!"

Hocine continued to dictate and the young worker wrote, against his will. Hocine had showed him a picture of Fatiha that she had slid between his shirts, and he had thought her beautiful, likeable and attractive with an extraordinarily present and questioning look. He, himself, would be very content to have a woman from back home at his side, as his adventures with French women always fell through without his really knowing why!

Hocine mailed the letter written at the work site himself. He was so irritated that he had torn up the wedding picture and now regretted it. One does not tear up a picture . . . And now, after the anger, after his heated reaction, came a certain uneasy feeling. He had done everything so that life at home and life here would not interfere with each other, and now they did, in spite of his efforts, and because Fatiha only does what she wants.

He sat down at the café below his hotel; he had not eaten, he was not hungry. The workers were playing cards and dominoes as usual, enthusiastic, vehement. He remained alone, in the back of the bar, drinking a beer, then a second, then a third, smoking cigarette after cigarette. He thought of Fatiha a lot more often than he would have liked. The letter . . . His parents . . . Fatiha's look. The look of his young friend at the work site.

Some musicians came in the café; they were welcomed with friendly shouts and applause. The men stood around them, requesting their favorite songs. The musicians tuned their instruments, laughed and played. Darbouka, tamborine, flute, like at his wedding...The men began to dance. How Mohamed had danced at his wedding!

At the other end of the room another man, alone, drank a beer too, but he seemed to be completely indifferent to the good mood of everybody around him. Hocine looked at him and it was if he were looking at himself, in front of his glass of beer, alone. So he got up, went upstairs and lay in bed. In the café the men continued to listen, dance and to recreate their own world through the music.

The next day Hocine woke up with the feeling that his whole weekend would be ruined by this letter. He could not put it out of his mind. He preferred to be alone with his bad humor. He went for a walk towards Clichy because he liked the flavor of this neighborhood. He hesitated in front of a movie theater, but none of the movies really interested him, neither the Egyptian films, nor the Bruce Lee films, nor the porno films, nor the other films...so he continued to walk. He caught sight of a young woman of Arab origin, standing before a shop window; he watched her; she appealed to him; he walked towards her and spoke to her; the young woman recoiled and quickly walked away. Hocine watched her walk away; a car stopped; she got in and pointed Hocine out to the driver, her friend? her husband? Hocine moved on quickly, turning down the first street. The driver accelerated to better insult him; fortunately Hocine had gone up a one way street and he couldn't turn.

Unhappy over this incident, he went into a café and ordered a beer and began smoking. Smoke...Drink a beer...A woman sat down near him and spoke to him.

"Come with me, come, as if we had all our lives before us; come, I like you..."

She smiled at him; he thought she was beautiful and womanly. A whore? A neglected wife? She put her hand on his leg. It was nice. Whore? Or just a sad woman? There was sadness in her look and this suited him just fine. She had blue eyes and red hair; she was wearing a long dress which looked like the ones worn by women in his country. He drank another beer; she drank a whiskey. He didn't quite know how much time they had spent there, and once they had left, how long they had been walking, holding hands as if they had known each other forever, nor how many floors they had walked up.

"Come on, my dear, I like you; come on, we have all the time in the world..."

She was a whore...; this gentleness, she was a woman...neglected...

"You make love well, my dear. Too bad! We won't be able to see each other again! Ah, how you appeal to me! I like it...I like it...and you...do you like it?"

Yes, he liked his pleasure, his freedom, their pleasure. He liked her lips, her body, her pubic hairs, almost black. Why do the women of my country pluck them? He liked these humid hairs. "Thank you woman! Thank you!"

"What did you say, my dear? Thank you? It's good... yes...it's good..."

They fell asleep together after sharing the body's greatest passion; then they went back downstairs holding each other's hand as if they loved each other very much and did not want to part. They had a coffee and separated.

"Too bad, my dear, that we can't see each other again!"

He had asked no questions.

Next day, a French worker came up to Hocine a few feet from the construction site.

"How's it going?"

"All right!"

"And the weekend?"

"All right!"

"I was lucky. . . but not at the tracks!"

He laughed.

"I met a woman. . . "

The French worker brought his hand to his mouth, all his fingers together on his lips, forming a kiss of admiration.

"It's not always Christmas like that. . . "

Hocine laughed.

"And me, I took a woman from my own country for a whore!"

The worker looked at Hocine, then lowered his eyes.

"Ah, my man, it's the mind. . . It's all in the mind!"

They arrived at the work site. Hocine was thinking of the young redheaded woman with the blue eyes. He would have liked so much to see her again.

When he saw his young friend he thought again of Fatiha's letter, of his anger, of his answer. He didn't for a minute doubt his response. It was the right answer. With her kind of person, only an answer like that could keep her quiet.

When his young friend wanted to talk to him about it during the lunch break, Hocine sent him packing the same way he had done with Allaoua:

"Mind your own business!"

But Karim was not angry with him; he did not understand Hocine very well, but he liked him a lot; you could count on him, take him at his word; he was always willing to help; he knew about life and never used his experience to exercise power over someone else; why was he like that with his young wife?

Hocine chased the memory of Fatiha and the letter from his mind. He thought about this young woman he had met by chance and who had a body so marvelously made for love. But was it only the body? All that tenderness? Where did she come from? Where did this woman come from? Who was she? What was the story of her life? Why had she chosen him? How did she get to that state? When two bodies find each other they should never separate. But was it only two bodies?

It wasn't just the openness of that body he would remember, but the tenderness, the trust, the respect. . . yes. . . that respect. . . not a word, not a look, not a gesture had hurt him. . . '

Hocine's letter arrived at home. And as usual his parents asked Allaoua to read it. It was written in Arabic and Allaoua read it slowly to himself first.

"We're listening, son."

"It's difficult to read."

"You should try to read our language a little bit better! It's no use going to school so long. . ."

"Writing is not always so easy to make out."

Allaoua discovered the content of the letter; imagining immediately the consequences it would have, he decided to alter it.

"He says he is doing well, he thinks a lot of you, he is working hard, that you have to work hard in France now if you want to keep your job, because there's a lot of unemployment. He says that it's cold in Paris, and that he will do everything possible to come back here for the birth, but he can't promise, given the situation where he works."

Aïcha, moved, listened, happy. Yamina went to get Fatiha, who came in quickly. Allaoua looked at her, then fixed his attention back on the letter.

"He says he will write more soon."

"He's a good son! He is brave! He respects his parents, his family! May God be praised!"

"May he soon be among us and not leave again! If Alla

wills it!" answered Amor, and he turned towards Allaoua. "And you learn to read our language more fluently!"

Allaoua laughed. Fatiha hurriedly left the room.

Fatiha, who had been putting her things away in the wardrobe when Yamina had come to get her, picked them up violently and threw them across the room.

Allaoua knocked at the door, using their code.

"Come in!"

He entered, saw everything on the floor, then looked at Fatiha.

"You came to tell me something? Well, say it!"

Allaoua hesitated again, and then looked her straight in the eyes.

"It's that. . . I did not read what was in the letter at all."

"Well, tell me what was written."

Her tone of voice was sharp, her face hard. Allaoua, startled, hesitated again, worried.

"Are you going to speak?"

"Hocine did receive your letter. He's furious. He complained to my parents; he said you don't have any right to be giving him orders, and that you are not to write him without our parents knowing about it. If I had read that, there would have been a scene, can you imagine. . ."

"But read them this letter, Allaoua! You would have done better to read it to them! Read it to them! Give it to me, I'm going to read it to them and everything will be clearer!"

"I don't have the letter any more; you know my mother always puts them to her heart; and then in her pocket!"

"That's good; that way they will read it one day; they'll know what's in it. I'm fed up, Allaoua, if only you knew how fed up I am living like this! I wanted to speak to Hocine because we are husband and wife according to the wishes of our parents, because we're expecting a child; but he is no different from his mother and father. For them, for him, I only exist in terms of what they expect from me, in what they want me to be, not for what I am, not for what I want to be! I can't stand it any more; it's more than I can take. I'll go crazy! I saw crazy women at the hospital. . . "

There was such a degree of intensity in Fatiha's words, such a powerful rejection in her whole being, such a fierce emotion, that Allaoua saw the irreversibility of Fatiha's words. This vehemence, this rebellion, worried and pleased him at the same time. He knew for sure that his eldest brother would not give in to Fatiha, and even if he had remained here, at home, the differences between him and his wife would not have been mitigated; without a doubt they would have gotten worse. He knew that it was very difficult for men to change their way of thinking, their behavior. Everything was against it: education, society, habits, how easy it was, and vanity as well. Since he had been seeing Fatouma and a few of her friends, he understood better to what degree their aspirations threatened the long established order of things. It was so much easier, when one lost his footing a bit, to take refuge in the established order; it was an answer to fear, to insecurity. What would it have taken to enable Hocine and Fatiha to simply talk to each other, to try to understand each other and the situation they were in? He spoke freely with Fatouma but everything did not become easy simply because one could speak freely. One had to go beyond that. . . You had to know your own strengths and your limitations. When you are one of those who have power over others, you have to learn to no longer want your own privileges. . . it was so difficult. . . Allaoua's extreme sensibility, his numerous contradictions, these family conflicts, this attraction towards his sister-in-law's personality—now transferred to her friend Fatouma—had helped him to make giant strides recently; but the ground was still very fragile under his feet; his enthusiasm, his lack of maturity, all too often still made him collide with reality, when what he wanted so much was to participate in transforming it.

"Leave me alone, Allaoua! Leave me alone!" Fatiha almost yelled.

Allaoua hesitated, then, afraid of a scandal, left with one idea in mind: get the letter from his mother's pocket and destroy it, to limit the damage and so gain time.

Left by herself, Fatiha again took her anger out on the things spread around her floor. Aïcha entered without knocking, she must have heard Fatiha's yelling. She saw the linen on the floor, trampled, and her daughter-in-law's expression frightened her. Fatiha crossed in front of her and walked out without a word. Aïcha, petrified, collapsed on the mattress; her legs no longer supported her. "Oh... la...la...la...la... how mistaken we were!" The little ones, who were looking for her, came running in.

"Mama, Néfissa stole my telephone!"

"Néfissa, will you give the telephone back to your brother!"

Néfissa ran away yelling; she did not want to "give back" the telephone, because it had been given to her... and, at that precise moment, she needed to feel like its exclusive owner!

"You have the devil in you, I swear! What is happening in this house? It would be better to die than to see this!"

Aïcha got up with difficulty and left the room, extremely tired.

In the sleepless night that followed, she was absolutely certain that the only thing possible was to go pray at the shrine of Sidi Hissa and, with her usual application, she concentrated her thoughts, her imagination, her energy, on this little expedition which suddenly took on the power to resolve everything and finally restore the family and religious order.

Two days later Aïcha walked across the courtyard very

early in the morning, dignified, in the brand new cloak that Amor had brought the night before.

"I'll be back before this evening."

"Go in peace, woman! Go in peace!" Amor told her. He knew where she was going. He held back the little ones who ran after their mother as usual, and he very attentively gave them multicolored pieces of paper and taught them how to make flying feathers. The children followed their father's motions, fascinated. Fatiha was preparing to wash the courtyard and Yamina began cleaning up the living room.

During the whole journey, Aïcha looked very little at the magnificent view that led to the holy place, completely absorbed in the task to be accomplished. She went as far as possible by bus and got out by herself in the middle of the country. She stood still for a minute, holding her well stocked basket in her right hand, and she looked up at the shrine way on top of the hill, set among prickly pear trees, olive trees over one hundred years old, pine trees, and aloes. She started up the path, which was difficult to negotiate because the stones rolled under one's feet and each step raised the dust from the dry earth. She went up, heavy yet light, her veils floating in the breeze, muttering incantations and looking, from time to time, at the little white mosque under the sun high in the sky; it was hot; she stopped to wipe her face, and began her ascent and incantation again. She met a little girl coming down from the shrine, holding a large black stone in her hands. Aïcha looked at the child, the little girl did not look at her. Aïcha stopped again to catch her breath, wiped her face, then continued to walk.

Once she arrived at the foot of the little mosque, she stopped a moment and then went in. It was dark and cool. Women were praying; most of them were old. Aïcha kissed the walls covered with banners, and walked around the tomb over which hung multicolored scarves. New candles just placed next to others, half or completely burned, lit up the emblems the women could not read. Aïcha lay out her mat, put her basket before her, took out the scarves and candles which she spread on the mat. Incense, burning in little niches in the walls, profusely dispersed in the air, provoked coughs that mixed with the litanies. Aïcha got up, put down her offerings, silk scarves, sugar, coffee, then approached an old woman, a direct descendant of the marabout, sitting in an adjoining room. Aïcha bowed; the old woman prayed. Aïcha came back to her mat, threw coins in the different corners of the mosque, then sat down and fervently launched into an improvised prayer, among all these women who also hoped that their most cherished wishes would come true.

"Ya Sidi, I have come to visit you to implore your power. Make it so my son Hocine comes back and never leaves our country again! That he finds work here! That he stays with us, with his wife, with his child to be born!

"I implore you, Ya Sidi, chase away the evil spirits tormenting my daughter-in-law, and that are now tormenting my own children! Ya Sidi Aïssa, I am your dog, your servant, I am your faithful one! Ya Sidi Aïssa, help me! I throw myself at your feet! I ask you your forgiveness! Your servant, Ya Sidi Aïssa, is suffering in her body and in her soul! Things are not right in the family, things are not right!"

Aïcha raised her arms, lowered them, then crossed them over her breast.

"I don't know what to do any more, Ya Sidi Aïssa. I am here, do you hear me? I am here. My eldest son has gone back to France and he has left us this woman; and ever since, everything has been going wrong at the house; the son disobeys his father, the father beats his son! I can't take any more! Help me! Help us! I promise you a 'waada', only for you, next month! I will slay a lamb; I'll make a coucous! Sidi Aïssa! Sidi Aïssa! I am your dog! Help me! You can do it!"

All around her the women prayed with the same fer-

vor; some coming in, others going out. Aïcha remained
another moment on her mat, in meditation, spent; then she
got up slowly, wrapped herself in her cloak, picked up her
mat and her basket and left. Outside, the great heat and the
intensity of the light hit her, she squatted in front of the
wall of the little mosque, picked up some sand, put a pinch
on her forehead, carefully put the rest in a handkerchief,
and just as carefully put the handkerchief in her basket; she
got up and slowly walked away, majestically, completely
illuminated by her faith and the rites she had just performed with confidence, with all her soul, with all her
heart. The grasshoppers sang to the hot earth and sun. The
little girl sat in the shade of a pine tree on the side of the
road, holding the black rock tight against her stomach; she
watched Aïcha pass, and Aïcha smiled to her, relieved; she
walked carefully so as not to fall; she thought of the bus she
had to catch, of the distance to travel to get home before
dark.

———————————

Fatiha found out from Allaoua that Aïcha had gone to
pray to chase away the evil spirits, and the gap separating
them widened a bit more. Under the pretext of fatigue, she
shut herself in her room. She would not be present at
Aïcha's return. She lay down but could not go to sleep, she
got up and walked back and forth in the room, her hair undone, her two hands on her stomach, on her child. She felt
certain that here nothing short of her total submission
would ever be possible, her acceptance of everything that is
considered correct, necessary and unchangeable; nothing
other than her assimilation. But she now knew that she
was incapable of this, totally incapable. What could she do?
Leave? To go where? She needed air; she threw a shawl over

her shoulders and walked into the courtyard. All the lights were off. The house was calm. All around, everything was silent. Fatiha leaned against the fig tree, then walked along the wall, leaning up against it from time to time; then she put her face against the stone, her hands on the wall as if to push it. She banged her forehead against it several times and remained still a long while. She did not think any more, it was a moment of unleashing images, of memories, of disorganized ideas; in her body and spirit, it was like a large violent wave looking for a shoreline where it could be calmed. The baby moved. Fatiha again began walking in the night with the sky full of stars overhead, so vast. Then she went back in, tired of walking. Exhausted by the emotion, she lay down and went to sleep.

When she woke up the next morning, she had the impression she had seen in her dream an old and charming cousin who, the day of her wedding, had noticed her sadness, and that she had heard the words she had said with a smile: "You have to smile at life, my angel, if you don't it will shrivel up like an old goat skin in the sun."

You have to smile at life...

She wanted to do it but she could not when her deepest urges were denied, when what was demanded of her condemned her to obedience and silence.

You have to smile at life... You have to leave...

Leave.

Aïcha and Yamina were sitting in the courtyard eating breakfast from the tray.

"We forgot to tell father to drop by the electrician's to see about the TV; we could do without it anyway... the children don't learn anything good from it! Why hasn't Fatiha come for breakfast yet? Go see..."

Yamina got up, but at that same moment Fatiha came out of her room, dressed like she were going for a walk, but without her veil. She smiled affectionately at Yamina and kissed her. Aïcha looked at her without understanding, but already troubled.

"Where are you going? What are you doing?"

"I'm leaving!"

Aïcha jumped up, knocked over the cups that broke, brutally pushed away Yamina who had remained fixed, dazed, with tears in her eyes, and stood in front of the door. She grabbed Fatiha by the arm and stopped her from going out.

"Fatiha, if you leave the house like this you'll never set foot in here again! Go back to your room immediately!"

Fatiha broke away with unsuspected strength and opened the outside door. Aïcha held her back by her dress. Fatiha went out.

"Don't leave! You'll be a cursed woman!"

Yamina watched the scene, transfixed, distraught, paralyzed.

"Hocine, my son, why did you leave again? Oh, what a disaster! What a disaster!"

Aïcha abandoned the idea of running after Fatiha; she closed the outside door and almost ripped her clothes off, suffocating. The little ones came running, then stopped in front of their mother and looked at her, not comprehending. Yamina, still standing in the same place, was crying.

Fatiha walked with determination, not paying attention to the street or what was happening in it; she walked, carried by a surprising strength, almost a second state of being.

She passed Radia's house. Radia saw Fatiha walking without her veil. With her pace, and the expression on her face, she guessed the scene. For an instant she thought of running to catch up with her, but Fatiha had already turned the corner and Radia, intuitively, understood that something permanent was taking place, over which she had no power. But she was afraid because she knew that Fatiha risked losing herself and that without help, without money, without the possibility of finding work, the woman who left her family in this way, if she is not accepted back by her parents-in-law, or shut in by her own parents, if she is not a victim of the desperate excesses of tradition, risks exhausting herself in a merciless struggle.

Fatiha walked quickly towards her parents' house, in spite of the weight in her stomach and the pain that took her breath away.

When she arrived at her parents' on the other side of Algiers, exhausted from the fast walk and the nervous emotion, Houria was sewing. When she opened the door and saw her daughter, without a veil, the expression on her face, she remained motionless, taken aback, stupefied.

"Fatiha, my child, what's the matter?"

Fatiha, overcome by dizziness, slowly fell to the floor.

"My God! My God, you didn't dishonor us?"

Fatiha got up with difficulty, breathed deeply, ran her hand across her face, leaned on the door handle.

"I will never go back there!"

She had said it with violence. Houria was overwhelmed and paralyzed:

"Fatiha, you have dishonored us!"

Then she began to cry. Fatiha gathered all her strength to leave.

Leave. Leave.

But she did not have the strength; she fell again, exhausted.

"I did not want this! I did not want to leave my husband! But I cannot live like in the old days... I want to be able to raise my child my way... Life... is not..."

She fainted.

Fatiha was taken to the hospital and the baby, a little girl, was born prematurely but was doing well. When Fatiha learned that it was a girl, she thought it was good, since her husband's family and he himself expected a boy, wanted a boy; they would suffer less and would leave her with her child with less regret.

A few days later when she realized what she had done, she was at times seized by panic and, to calm her fears for the future, she dreamed that her husband joined her, that he agreed to live a different life with her, but reality was completely the opposite. Aïcha, convinced that Fatiha was possessed by a demon, and so deeply possessed that her prayers and offerings were of no effect, thought, once her emotion and anger had passed, that it was better this way and that it was God's will.

Amor spent a few days of great anger as well, and thought about going to get Fatiha as soon as possible, to force her to give in, to bring her back to the house, to her duty under the family order; but Hocine, who had been informed immediately, called his father at work and told him: "Let her go!" Let her go... and Amor prayed to God that his will be done!

Let her go! Hocine did not want to keep Fatiha by force. He had not wanted to marry, but he had married her and she was expecting a child... Let her go... He had to live through another rupture. He suffered... He had been thinking of his son recently...

Let her go! Once again alone. He no longer had a wife at home...

But had he ever stopped being alone?

Fatiha was not alone, the child was on the pillow at her side. She wanted to name her Noura, in memory of Noura who had been so marvelously present when she was in the hospital, who had so much understanding of life, and also because Nour meant the light. . .

She caressed the baby's cheeks with her fingers. "My angel, my beautiful one, my little spring, my light, you must not cry, there are so many joys to come for you! You are going to walk, you are going to run, you are going to talk, you are going to swim in the sea! You are going to sing! You'll see the palm trees in the sun, the stars at night, the oranges on the tree, you'll pick them and eat them! You'll eat prickly pears and watermelons, pink like your tongue. You must not cry, my beautiful!"

The nurse cracked the door open. She listened to the mother and smiled.

"You have a visit!"

She opened the door wide and Leila, Myriem, Zahra and Fatouma came in with their arms full of flowers, gifts for the baby, and with all their friendship in their eyes, in their smiles, in their hearts. And because they were there, Fatiha knew tomorrow would be less difficult.

Ali Ghalem (also sometimes spelled Ghanem), an Algerian filmmaker, has made three feature-length films in France, including a screen version of *A Wife For My Son*. He has won the silver medal at the Verona film festival and the Special Judges Prize of the Prades Festival. *A Wife For My Son* won an award at Venice. His most recent novel to be published in the U.S. is *The Seven-Headed Serpent*.